WILD IRISH SOUL

BOOK 3 IN THE MYSTIC COVE SERIES

TRICIA O'MALLEY

LOVEWRITE PUBLISHING

WILD IRISH SOUL

BOOK 3 IN THE MYSTIC COVE SERIES

"Art is the stored honey of the human soul." ~ Theodore Dreiser

CHAPTER 1

"*A*ISLINN, WAIT!"

Aislinn swore under her breath as Baird yelled to her from the door of Gallagher's Pub. Pasting on a polite smile, she turned to face him.

Baird Delaney.

Tall, dark and yum is how Cait had described him and Aislinn couldn't agree more. Or maybe it was the wire-framed glasses that had sunk her. Baird had come into her shop earlier in the week to pick up some art for his new psychiatry office and Aislinn's world had shifted.

"Sorry, Baird, I didn't mean to duck out, but I've had a long week," Aislinn said smoothly as she clenched her fingers around her purse. All of Baird's heat and glow seemed to pulse at her and it was almost like looking into the sun. Aislinn squinted and put her mental shields up, trying to act normal.

"Ash...sorry, can I call you that?" Baird stopped and asked politely, twisting Aislinn's heart even further.

"Sure, thanks for asking," Aislinn said demurely and

tried not to look directly at his smoky gray eyes fringed by the darkest lashes she'd ever seen. To keep her mind from the tight body packed into the black t-shirt he wore, Aislinn tried to place a name to the color of his eyes. Graphite? No, too dark. Slate? No, still too dark. Sleet.

"Ash? Hello?"

Startled from her thoughts, Aislinn blushed. And then wanted to kick herself for blushing. She never got like this.

"Sorry, what were you saying?"

A slow smile crept across Baird's face, almost as if he knew where her train of thought had gone.

"I wanted to know where you were going. It isn't that late."

"Ah, well, you know, running a business can be taxing; I wanted to get up early to finish some projects," Aislinn said in a rush of breath.

"But the main band hasn't started yet. I was hoping that you would dance with me," Baird said and stepped closer to Aislinn. His nearness was like a punch to the gut, and Aislinn felt a little dizzy. She did her best not to step back.

"Another night," Aislinn whispered, trying her best not to stare at his mouth.

"Am I reading this wrong? I was quite certain that there was an attraction here," Baird said directly and Aislinn jumped. Leave it to a psychiatrist to be forward with his feelings, she thought.

"I just…I just have to…" Aislinn trailed off lamely as she stared into his face. His very essence seemed to hypnotize her and helpless to stop herself, she closed the distance between them and brushed a kiss across his lips.

A flash of heat, of rightness, seared her and Aislinn stumbled back quickly.

"Oh no you don't," Baird said quietly and grabbed her arms, pulling her close until her breasts brushed against his hard chest.

Aislinn trembled against Baird as he took her lips with his own, nibbling ever so softly. She sighed into his mouth as he seduced her with his kiss, coaxing her to open up to him, to give just a little more. Soon, she found herself all but wrapped around him as their kiss intensified. Aislinn moaned into his mouth just as a wolf whistle broke their embrace.

Unable to look at the person who whistled, Aislinn stared at Baird's chest, happy to see that it was heaving just as much as hers was. She couldn't bring herself to meet his eyes. Neither said a word.

Reaching a decision, Aislinn sighed and took his hand. "Take me home with you."

"What? No. I'd like to take you on a date is what I'd like to do," Baird said stiffly, his honor clearly offended. For some reason, it delighted Aislinn and she laughed up into his handsome face.

"By the book, are you?"

"Not always, but in this instance, yes," Baird said.

"Don't you want to live a little, Doctor?" Aislinn said and raised an eyebrow at him. She was enchanted when she saw a blush heat *his* cheeks.

"It's not that I don't want to live a little, it's that I want you to take me seriously," Baird said quietly.

"Oh, I promise I'll take you seriously. Very seriously,"

Aislinn whispered and leaned in to nip at Baird's bottom lip.

Baird sighed and rested his forehead against hers.

"You know that I want you," Baird whispered.

"I know," Aislinn said.

"But, this feels wrong," Baird said.

"It isn't. It will be right. So right," Aislinn said and smiled up at him. Aislinn was surprised at herself. As an artist and a woman supremely confident in her own being, she wasn't necessarily free with the partners that she chose to share her bed with, yet at the same time, she wasn't opposed to starting something up when an attraction was evident. Rarely, though, did she move this fast – with anything in her life.

"My place is in shambles, I've barely unpacked. Shouldn't we go to yours?" Baird asked; resignation warred with excitement in his voice.

"No, let's go to yours. We'll make you feel at home," Aislinn said with a laugh. She wasn't ready to let Baird into her home. Very few were invited up to her apartment, her haven, and Aislinn was certain that if Baird went there with her it would be dangerously hard to erase the memory of him in her space.

"On one condition," Baird said.

Aislinn tilted her head up at him and waited.

"I get to take you on a real first date. A nice one, like adults, where we do all the first date stuff and get to know each other better," Baird said firmly.

Aislinn smiled up at Baird despite the worry that ran through her. Oh, yeah, she could easily fall for him.

"Deal."

CHAPTER 2

*A*ISLINN'S PALM WARMED in Baird's large hand as he pulled her down the sidewalk with him towards his office and apartment overlooking the harbor. The sounds of the small village settled around them and Aislinn took a deep breath to settle her sudden nerves. So sure of herself seconds ago, now she wondered what she was doing.

It wasn't the sex that scared her. It was the after. The date that she had promised to go on. Aislinn shook her head. What she should do was run far away from Baird. There was no way that this proper doctor and her were ever going to work out in a real relationship.

"Nice night," Baird said and Aislinn jumped.

"Yes, it is," she said as he laughed at her.

"You know, this was your idea," Baird teased her and Aislinn caught herself laughing up at him.

"I know. I'm being ridiculous. Tell me why you moved your practice here," Aislinn said to deflect the conversation from what they were about to go do. She could all but see a neon sign blinking SEX in her head.

"I needed a change. I love Galway, but something called me here. I've been here several times. Take a long weekend, drive down the coast, stare at the water. I don't know how to explain it. I just needed to be in Grace's Cove. I saved a bunch of money from my practice and decided to take a hiatus down here. I can't imagine that my practice will be as busy as in Galway but I'm sure that I'll eventually be able to build up a clientele. If not, well, I'll cross that road when I get to it," Baird said and shrugged.

Aislinn wondered if the cove really was what had called him. It wouldn't be the strangest thing that had happened in this town.

"I wouldn't be surprised if you have a bustling practice here," Aislinn mused.

"You think? I often find with small towns that people are reluctant to try therapy of any sort," Baird said eagerly, the passion for his business lacing his voice.

"Oh, I'm certain you'll find Grace's Cove to be unlike most small towns that you know," Aislinn laughed softly.

"You'll have to explain that sometime. I'd love to learn more about this town," Baird said, raising an eyebrow as they approached his building.

"Well, I'm sure you've heard all sorts of rumors," Aislinn began and Baird stopped her.

"Another time," Baird insisted and pulled her hand to his heart before leaning down to brush a kiss over her lips. Aislinn felt a warm ball of lust begin to pulse low in her stomach.

Baird turned and slipped the key into the lock on his

door, pulling Aislinn along with him into the small stair-well that led to the second floor.

"The apartment isn't much, but the view was worth it," Baird said as they climbed the worn wooden stairs.

"I can imagine. I'm in love with the water here," Aislinn said and bumped into Baird's back as he stopped and turned to look at her.

"In love with it? Interesting phrase," Baird said.

"Don't think too deeply about it, Dr. Delaney." Aislinn smiled up at him though her head swarmed with thoughts. She supposed it was part of his job, to analyze underlying meanings.

"I'm not. Just interesting. There's a serious difference between loving something and being in love," Baird said as he continued down the hallway to a small door painted a cheerful red. Aislinn leaned against the wall and watched Baird as he unlocked the door.

"I suppose there is, then," Aislinn said softly.

Baird met her eyes before pushing the door open.

"Welcome," he said and gestured for her to step into his home.

Aislinn brushed past Baird and felt a shiver run over her body at his nearness. She was trying hard to keep her mental shields up, but Baird just seemed to pulse with a heady combination of lust, intelligence, and warmth. She took a deep breath as she walked across his small living room to stand at the window.

"The moon is bright tonight," Aislinn said.

Baird kept the light off and walked across the room to join her at the window. Aislinn trembled as he stepped behind her and looked over her shoulder at the water that spread before them.

"Aye, it is at that. Just look at that sky," Baird said.

The moon hung like a fat globe in the sky, its soft white light tracing a path across the calm water of the harbor. Stars winked along the horizon and Aislinn ached to paint the romance of the harbor.

"If I painted this, I would call it Mermaid's Light," Aislinn mused.

"That's sweet. What would you paint it in?"

"Probably watercolors. Just to get that fine blurring at the edges…see where the sky meets the line of the water and how they blend softly together? Watercolors would be perfect for that," Aislinn said.

"Blending. I like that. Isn't that sort of what we are doing here?" Baird asked. Aislinn jumped a bit as he ran his hands down her arms before circling her waist. Nerves kicked in for a moment but she blew out a breath. There was no denying her attraction for Baird, but he carried with him the threat of a real relationship. One which Aislinn wasn't certain she could handle. But, if tonight was all she was going to allow herself with him then she was going to go all in, Aislinn thought.

Aislinn turned in Baird's arms and looked up at him from under her eyelids.

"There hasn't been much blending going on as of yet, has there?" Aislinn said cheekily and Baird huffed out a soft laugh before pulling her tight against his chest.

Aislinn gasped as her breasts brushed the hard muscles of his chest. Though he was brainy as all get out, Baird had clearly not neglected his body. Aislinn imagined that more than one of his patients had a crush on him. Moonlight slashed across his face, highlighting the intensity in his eyes. Aislinn met his gaze. A strong surge of lust snapped between them.

Baird shook his head and stared down at her mouth. "You shouldn't be beautiful."

Aislinn's mouth dropped open and she smacked him on the chest but he held her tight to him.

"Your face. It's a mixture of all of these really interesting contrasting elements. It shouldn't work but it does. It could stop a man at ten paces."

Aislinn gaped at him, lost in his words, in the lust and light that emanated from him.

"You're not so bad yourself, Dr. Yum," Aislinn said with a smile.

Baird's eyebrows drew together in confusion. "Dr. Yum?"

Aislinn laughed and stretched up to nip his bottom lip. "Yum," she purred.

"Ah," Baird said as he brushed his lips softly across hers and Aislinn felt heat build low in her belly. She slid her hands up his chest and wrapped them around his neck. Pulling his head closer, Aislinn poured herself into the kiss. She allowed her shields to drop and Baird's feelings washed over her. It was like his lust punched her in the gut and Aislinn staggered against his lips. Lust, tinged with a hint of yearning. Aislinn's heart did a little spin at the thought and she desperately tried to stay focused on the physical sensations that Baird was building in her body.

"You taste like the moon…cool heat," Baird murmured against her lips.

"Ah, a poet you are," Aislinn said as Baird began to walk backwards with her in his arms.

"A hobby," Baird admitted. He turned and pulled her down a dark hallway towards the bedroom. He moved through a doorway and bent to switch on a small table lamp that sat on the floor in the corner. Boxes lined the room and a king bed dominated the rest of the small space.

Scared that Baird would back out – that she would lose this one night with him – Aislinn stepped to Baird and pushed him backwards towards the bed until the back of his legs hit the bed.

Nudging him gently until he sat back on the mattress, Aislinn met his eyes before reaching down and pulling the hem of her dress over her head. Satisfaction filled her when Baird's mouth dropped open at the sight of her bright purple lace bra and thong. Though Aislinn wasn't overweight, she also wouldn't throw herself in the slim category either. She had enough curves to make her purple lace interesting and when Baird immediately reached his hands out to cup her breasts, she smiled. Purple lace for the win, she thought.

"Sweet Jesus," Baird whispered as he cupped her breasts in his hands. Aislinn shivered as he brushed his thumbs over her nipples.

"I like colorful underwear," Aislinn said.

"And for that, I thank you," Baird said. Aislinn shrieked as he scooped her up and tossed her on the bed. Bouncing once, her hair tumbled down from its pin and she glared up at him from under a mop of curls. Her mouth dropped open as Baird stripped his shirt off and stood before her in his fitted jeans and glasses.

Pushing her hair out of her face she glared at him. "Real smooth."

Baird laughed and unbuckled his jeans, peeling them down muscular legs. Aislinn gaped at his boxer briefs, where his desire for her was clearly evident. Baird climbed onto the bed and kneeled over her, bracing his arms on either side of her shoulders.

Leaning down to nip at her bottom lip, Baird winked at her. "While I appreciate that you are a strong, modern woman, I like to do the seducing, Aislinn."

A shot of pure heat streaked through her and Aislinn's mouth dropped open as he ducked his head to capture her nipple through the lace, teasing it into a taut peak. She moaned as he worked his mouth over her breasts, arching her back to give him better access. Frustrated with the barrier of lace, she reached behind her and released her breasts from the confines of the bra.

Baird moaned as she slipped the bra off and threw it on the floor. He captured her breasts in his large hands and continued to rub her nipples as his mouth worked its way down her soft stomach. A scatter of nerves shot through her as she realized where he was going. Baird's breath was hot against her stomach and he reached down to tug at the slim strap of lace that covered her right hip.

Baird sliced a glance at her. "How attached to these are you?"

"I love them."

"I'll buy you another pair." Aislinn's mouth went dry as Baird tore the lace from her body. Baird smiled wickedly at her and moved himself between her legs. She gasped as he bent his head to the V between her legs. Aislinn closed her eyes and allowed herself to be swept away by the emotional and physical sensations that pounded at her. With her mental shields down it was like she was in two places at once. Feeling Baird's lust as his tongue teased her to the point of orgasm was a powerful aphrodisiac. Help-less to stop the wave of sensations that rolled through her, Aislinn shouted to the ceiling as Baird took her over the edge into a searing heat. Aislinn gasped as her legs bucked around his head.

Baird leveraged himself up and kissed his way up her stomach, past her breasts before nuzzling into the soft spot at her neck. Aislinn wrapped her arms around his broad back and pulled him to her, craving the weight of his body.

"Aislinn, you…God. Your body. I want it all," Baird gasped into her neck.

"I want you too. So badly," Aislinn whispered and turned her head to catch his lips in a kiss.

"I…I'm not prepared for this," Baird admitted. It took Aislinn a moment to realize what he meant.

"Oh, I'm on the pill. Same time every morning. We're good." Aislinn smiled up at him, grateful that he was kind enough to ask.

Baird's eyes narrowed in lust as he realized his last barrier was gone. Aislinn gaped at him as he held himself up on one arm and slid his underwear down with the other, kicking it off of the bed. The strength of this man was phenomenal, she thought right before he slid his body between her legs and eased her knees open.

Baird bent over and captured her bottom lip in his, sucking gently. Pulling back, he bent his forehead to hers.

"I wanted this the minute that I saw you earlier this

week. I've never been so powerfully attracted to someone before," Baird said at her lips.

"Me...me too," Aislinn admitted nervously.

"I'll have to step up my game on our first real date." Baird smiled against her mouth and in one smooth movement, thrust deeply inside of her. Aislinn cried out into his mouth, clenching her muscles against the intrusion while her whole body cried out, "Yes!"

Baird didn't wait for her to get accustomed to his length. Instead, he picked up speed, almost seeming to sense that Aislinn was close to another orgasm. Holding on, and matching him thrust for thrust, Aislinn cried out into his mouth as she shattered around him. Her whole body shook with the power of the orgasm and her heart seemed to whisper, "Yes, this one."

Aislinn held on as Baird found his completion. Pulling him closer, she panted against his shoulder as all of the nerve endings in her body stood to attention. His hard body against her softness seemed like the perfect fit.

Her mind scrambled to understand what had just happened. This wasn't the first time that she'd had casual sex, though she didn't make a habit of it. So why did this feel anything but casual? Her heart pounded in her chest, mimicking the rhythm she felt from his. Beat for beat... they matched each other.

Overwhelmed, Aislinn put her shields up, detaching herself from him emotionally. She smiled against his shoulder and pressed a kiss to his neck.

Baird levered himself up and looked down at her. He'd lost his glasses along the way and the soft light cut across his strong cheekbones. His hair stood out all over the place and Aislinn vaguely remembered running her hands through it and clenching it.

"Where did you go?"

"What?"

"Just now…I felt like you pulled away," Baird said.

Aislinn gaped at him. There was no way that he could know about her or her power. How in the world could he feel her disconnect?

"I'm right here." Aislinn smiled at him.

Baird just raised an eyebrow at her.

"Would you stop? Thank you, that was amazing," Aislinn said.

"You're breathtaking," Baird said and bent to brush a soft kiss over her lips. Aislinn moaned as he moved from her and rolled to find his underwear.

"I'm going to get a glass of water. Do you want one?"

"Sure. Bathroom?"

Baird gestured to a door down the hallway and Aislinn watched him walk from the room in his boxer briefs, admiring the view.

"Shit, shit, shit," Aislinn said as she dropped back against the bed. Leaning over, she grabbed her bra and dress from the floor. Aislinn made a beeline for the bathroom to clean herself up a bit. Taking a quick glance in the mirror she sighed at how happy she looked. Bright eyes, a blush across her cheeks and her hair tumbling every which way made her look a little crazy and really sexy. Aislinn pulled her bra on and shimmied into her dress. Knowing that her hair was a total loss, she twisted it into a knot and left the bathroom.

Bypassing the bedroom, Aislinn found Baird in the

small kitchen with the glasses of water. Her mouth went dry at seeing him all but naked with his sexy glasses on. He turned to her and her heart dropped as his face fell.

"Going somewhere?"

"Um, well, it's late and I, uh, have to open the store in the morning," Aislinn finished lamely and lifted her hands. Baird put the glasses down and walked to her, pinning her against the cabinet.

"It's not that late, Aislinn," Baird said dangerously, his mouth inches from hers.

"I know…I just…I can't stay. Small towns, gossip, you know how it is," Aislinn said.

"No, I don't. Stay," Baird said stubbornly, his lips teasing hers.

"I, I can't," Aislinn whispered against his mouth.

"Why?" Baird demanded.

"Don't, Baird. I, this was great. Truly. Thank you for making it special," Aislinn said and moved from his arms. Reaching up, she gave him a light kiss and patted his cheek. "I'll see you around."

Baird watched her as she snagged her purse from the counter and walked to the door.

"What are you running from?"

Aislinn stopped with her hand on the doorknob. This was just as she feared. Dating a psychiatrist would mean that he would be able to see through all her smoke and mirrors to the true vulnerability that lay beneath it all. Certain she was in the right for leaving, Aislinn turned to look at him.

"Sleep well, Dr. Delaney."

CHAPTER 3

*B*AIRD WATCHED THE door close after Aislinn and his hand clenched around the glass of water. Striding across the living room, he stood at the window and watched her hurry down the street as though she couldn't get away from him fast enough.

"Damn it, Aislinn," Baird said as he placed his hands against the window. His eyes followed her red dress, standing out in the light of the streetlamps like a beacon, until she turned the corner.

What was she running from? Baird thought as he stared at the water. He'd never felt so connected to someone so quickly before. One-night stands weren't in his repertoire and it itched at him that she had just left like that after convincing him this was a good idea.

He'd protested, hadn't he? It wasn't like he had used her. In fact, Baird was dangerously close to assuming that he had just been used himself.

But.

There was something there. He knew it. He'd felt it the

moment that he had met her at her shop. He'd been captivated by the black-and-white photographs hanging in the window and had rushed eagerly into the shop to see what else the artist had. When Aislinn had turned from the canvas she had been working on in the back, her hair a mess of curls, paint smudges covering her smock, and had met his eyes…he'd been lost. It was like time had simply stopped for a moment. Had her cousin Cait not come into the shop shortly after, Baird was certain he would have done something foolish like ask to buy her a house…or to run away with him.

Baird shook his head and ran his hand through his hair. Moving from the window, he snagged the glass of water and walked back to the bedroom. Aislinn had responded instantly to his touch and he was certain that she had been just as satisfied as him. And, yet. There was that moment afterwards where he sensed that she was withdrawing… building up her boundaries. As a psychiatrist, he was trained to watch for those cues in his patients but it had surprised him that he could all but feel it from Aislinn. But, what had happened to make her step back from him? He'd already been planning on cooking her breakfast and snuggling up to her in his sheets.

Baird groaned as he flopped back against his covers, his hand landing on her lace thong. He held it up and twirled it around his finger. The delicacy of the lace belied the strength that its owner held. So, what was she running away for?

Challenges didn't scare Baird, and Aislinn had just moved to the top of his list to figure out. Determined to peel back her layers, Baird set to plotting.

CHAPTER 4

*a*ISLINN ALL BUT ran to her shop, the Wild Soul Gallery, desperate to get inside her sanctuary. What was she doing? Aislinn let out a stream of curses as she unlocked the back door of her shop and took the stairs two at a time to her apartment above the store. Flicking on the overhead lights, she crossed the cluttered living room to her kitchen to pull a bottle of Bulmer's from her refrigerator. Kicking off her shoes, Aislinn walked to her plush red couch and plopped down on the cushions to stare at the wall.

Decorated with her artwork, the room was a cacophony of color and mood. It was jarring and comforting at the same time, just the way that Aislinn liked it. She never wanted to get too comfortable…with anything in her life. If she knew one thing, it was that life could change in an instant.

Aislinn took a deep pull from the bottle and allowed the crisp cider to cool her throat. Deep down, she knew why she had run from Baird. Though there was no denying the attraction she felt for him, Aislinn just didn't think that they would last in a long-term relationship. And, Dr. Yum had commitment written all over him.

Aislinn sighed and tucked her legs under her. It wasn't that she couldn't commit to someone. She looked around the room at her half-finished art projects. Okay, so she sometimes had trouble committing to a project, but she had been in relationships before. It was just that she and Baird were so different.

And she knew where that would lead…divorce. Heartache.

She knew from firsthand experience as she had watched her parents go through it. Leaning back, Aislinn allowed her mind to go back to those awful years. She and her twin brother, Colin, had just entered into their teens when their parents had split. It had been a shock to everyone but her.

It had been impossible for Aislinn not to see that her parents were unhappy. She could literally feel the wall of unhappiness that radiated from them when they were in the same room together. Her mother Mary, much like her, had preferred to be a free spirit, always setting up day trips to the country, going to see local bands, and planning trips away on her own. Her father had been the levelheaded businessman. Sean ran his life on a schedule and his boat tour business thrived because of it. The two had been a poor match from the beginning and Aislinn had often wondered what had drawn them together.

Until she'd learned about her half-sister Keelin, and Keelin's mother, Margaret, shortly after the divorce.

She wasn't meant to know, but Aislinn couldn't help

sharing the news with her only confidant at that point, Colin. She'd discovered a letter that Mary had written to Sean about how Mary knew that Sean had never gotten over his true love and that she knew about the daughter Sean had with Margaret.

It had been like a knife to the heart.

Aislinn had packed her bags that night and gone to live with her mother while Colin had chosen to stay with Sean. For the following few years, Aislinn had barely spoken to Sean and tolerated, if not sometimes enjoyed, her mother's absentminded ways. It hadn't taken much for her to move out from Mary's house and decide to settle in Grace's Cove. Finding her shop had been a blessing, and when Aislinn realized that she could afford the rent, she had never looked back.

Her relationship with her father had grown stronger over the years since she had moved out of Mary's house. Unable to hold a grudge for long, and feeling like she had gained some wisdom as she had matured, Aislinn was finally able to see Sean's side of the story – though she still was determined to hate her unknown half-sister Keelin.

Until the day that Keelin showed up in her shop.

Whoo, that had been quite a punch to the gut. Aislinn had wanted to hate Keelin on principle alone. But, Aislinn's ability made her able to see that Keelin was just as nervous and scared as she was. Together, they had formed a fragile bond over their mutual otherworldly gifts. Through the past year they had grown to be close, just like sisters were meant to be.

Aislinn sighed and shook her head. It was amazing how things worked out.

Thinking of her power, she barked out a laugh as she imagined Baird's quizzical look if she tried to explain that she could read people's feelings, auras, and even got glimpses of the future sometimes. He'd probably run right out the door.

Aislinn had stopped running from herself a long time ago, though. Even though she had run from Baird tonight, if he wanted something more from her, she would just have to tell him what she was. That would most likely nip things in the bud fairly quickly.

Uncomfortable with the thought of losing Baird completely, but certain that she was on the right path, Aislinn headed for her bedroom. Shame niggled at her for her poor behavior tonight – it was rude to leave Baird like she had. Sighing, she crawled under the covers of her huge bed and pulled her eye mask out. Aislinn suspected that she would be delivering an apology in the morning.

CHAPTER 5

THE NEXT DAY, Aislinn sat down at her desk in the shop and ran through her figures. Sales were up this summer and she would need new inventory soon. Unfortunately, she had barely been able to paint this morning as planned. Awakening before the sun came up, Aislinn had gone to the hills to capture the sunrise over the water. A fitful night of sleep had left her drowsy and moody, and her work had turned out more melancholy than she had intended. Calling it quits, she had come back to the shop to deal with some paperwork before she opened for the day.

Aislinn twisted a pencil in her mass of curls to pull them off her shoulders and squinted down at a bill on her desk. A knock interrupted her thoughts and she leaned back in the chair to look out the front window.

Nobody was visible through the front window, so she stood and the knock repeated again – from the back door. Aislinn hurried to the back, assuming it was Keelin or Cait come for a quick visit before work. Swinging the door open, she stopped in her tracks.

Baird stood before her, a clutch of daisies in his hand, and her heart melted, just a bit.

"Baird!"

"Aislinn, since I didn't get to wake up with you, I thought that I would bring you breakfast," Baird said and gestured to her table in the courtyard. Aislinn gaped at the table, set with fat candles, scones, tea, and a bowl of fruit. Turning to look at him, she struggled for words.

"Say, 'Thank you, Baird,'" Baird said.

"Thank you, Baird," Aislinn said automatically and then caught herself. "No, seriously, thank you. Let me get water for those flowers." Aislinn hurried into the small kitchen at the back of the shop and pulled out a small vase deglazed in a cheerful blue and popped the daisies in. Admiring their charm, she placed them on her work table and went to join Baird in her small courtyard situated off the back of her shop.

Baird sat at the table, a navy t-shirt molded to his chest and his wire-framed glasses in place. Aislinn wanted to go sit on his lap and wrap her arms around his neck. Instead, she crossed the courtyard and sat on the bench across from him. Nerves laced her stomach and her finger beat a *tap-tap-tap* rhythm on the table.

"Scone?" Baird asked.

"Please," Aislinn said softly and allowed Baird to put a warm scone onto her plate and spoon clotted cream on the side. Without asking, he poured her a cup of tea. Aislinn cleared her throat.

"Listen, I…I'm sorry about last night. I shouldn't have run out like that. Thank you for a wonderful time."

"Why did you?" Baird asked.

"Why did I run?"

"Yes."

"I…a lot of things, I guess." Aislinn shrugged her shoulders and shoved a piece of scone in her mouth to keep herself from talking more.

"Start with the first and go from there," Baird suggested.

"Well, that, for one. You're a psychiatrist," Aislinn grumbled.

Baird laughed at her. "So?"

"So, so…you are supposed to be hard to figure out. Instead you are super direct and now I feel put on the spot."

Baird leaned forward and met her eyes and Aislinn found herself struggling to breathe as she stared into his gray eyes.

"I don't play games. I don't lie. And, I'm straightforward with my feelings. In everything that I do." Baird's voice held an intensity that made Aislinn shiver a bit. He had made love to her with that same intensity last night.

"See, that's what scares me. You're serious. About everything. And, I don't know if I can commit to us. You're a commitment guy," Aislinn protested.

"Well, it's not like I asked you to marry me, Aislinn. I asked you out to dinner," Baird said gently.

"I know. I get all that. It's just…" Aislinn trailed off as she thought about what she wanted to hit him with. Their differences? Her childhood? Her gift?

"Let me guess, you've been hurt before and are reluctant to try again?" Baird hazarded a guess and waved his scone at her.

"Something like that. My parents are divorced."

"Ah, a rare thing in Ireland. That had to have been hard," Baird said.

"It was. Incredibly so. Even more so when I found out that my father was still in love with another woman and that I had a half-sister living in Boston."

"Whooo." Baird let out a soft whistle. "That's a lot. How old were you?"

"Thirteen. Perfect time for me to become all dramatic and move in with my mother."

"Was it just the other woman that split them?"

"No, they were so different. He was – *is* – a steady businessman. Very regimented. Focused on career success. My mom is a free spirit. Wild, on the move, you never know what you will get with her. I love her dearly, but she can be a handful sometimes."

"And so you see that as us? I'm an uptight psychiatrist and you are the free spirit?" Baird got directly to the point.

"Exactly."

"So you can't be persuaded to see where our similarities lie?"

"I honestly don't know. There is some stuff that you may never be able to understand, Baird," Aislinn said softly and looked helpless into his eyes.

"Try me."

Aislinn sighed and took a sip of her tea. Where to start?

"What do you know of the rumors of Grace's Cove – the actual cove, not the village – being enchanted?"

"Oh, I've heard all sorts of things about it. I'd love to go down there sometime."

"But, what specifically?"

Baird leaned back and watched her carefully. "I've heard that the cove can glow sometimes. I've heard that many people are afraid to go there. There are rumors that Grace O'Malley, the famous pirate queen, lies there. And, I've heard whispers of special powers of the descendants."

"Ah-ha! So, you have heard about the special powers."

Baird shrugged a shoulder. "So? It isn't like Celtic mythology isn't chock full of mystical tales."

"But what if it isn't mythology? What if it is real?" Aislinn asked carefully.

Baird's hands stilled.

"Are you trying to tell me something, Aislinn?"

Aislinn took a deep breath. Now or never, she thought. Knowing how hard it had been for Keelin and Cait to get deep into a relationship before telling their men about their gifts, Aislinn decided to take the plunge.

"All female descendants of Grace O'Malley have an extra special gift. It manifests differently for each female. Intuition, healing powers, reading minds, empathic abilities…each woman has her own ability to deal with," Aislinn said nervously.

"Really? That's fascinating. I'm not sure that is scientifically possible. Do you believe in that?" Baird asked, his eyebrow raised.

"See, this is why we won't work. You are so science-minded," Aislinn said, and made a move to get up. Baird reached across the table and grabbed her arm.

"Sit. Please. I'm sorry if I upset you. You just said that with such conviction."

Aislinn sat and met Baird's eyes.

"I'm a descendant of Grace O'Malley."

CHAPTER 6

$\mathcal{A}$ISLINN LET DOWN her shields and allowed herself to feel Baird's emotions. Confusion, a little bit of anger, covered in disbelief pulsed at her. She shook her head. Aislinn should have expected this response. She'd received it in the past; it wasn't like this was anything new.

"You're telling me that you have some magickal power?" Baird's voice went a little high at the end and Aislinn sighed. If this was to be the end of it, at least she could be honest.

"Yes. Though it's not magick. It just is."

"What…what can you do?"

"I'm empathic. I can read people's feelings, I can tell if they are lying, and sometimes I get glimpses of the future. Oh, and I see auras too. Yours is blue. A lovely aura, in fact…" Aislinn trailed off as she watched Baird's face.

"I…I'm not really sure what to say."

Aislinn shrugged her shoulders. "It's okay. I know that you don't believe me."

"It's not that. I'm sure that you believe what you are saying."

A slap of anger hit Aislinn and she worked to control her breathing.

"I believe what I am saying because it's the truth."

"Okay, okay…I'm not calling you a liar," Baird said soothingly. Aislinn threw up her hands.

"Don't pull your shrink crap on me. I'm not crazy. This is the truth. And, this is why we can't date. You'll never accept it." She got up and stood in front of the table. "Thanks for breakfast. And for last night, sincerely. It was wonderful, but this can go nowhere."

Baird jumped up and walked around the table to face her. Aislinn's breath hitched at his nearness and she tried her best to act unaffected.

"You didn't exactly give me a lot of time to process what you just said, Aislinn," Baird said.

"What do you want? Evidence? Go ahead, tell me a truth or a lie," Aislinn dared him.

Baird sighed.

"I'm thirty-six years old."

"Lie."

Baird shook his head at her. "Okay, I'm thirty-three."

"Truth," Aislinn said.

"My mom lives in Galway."

"Truth."

"I'm wearing black underwear."

"False. Are we done here? I need to open my shop," Aislinn said angrily and turned away only to be whipped around.

Baird crushed his lips to hers and Aislinn pushed at his

chest. Caught in his arms, she melted against him. Just for a minute. When he loosened his arms, Aislinn stepped back, tamping down the lust that rose deep inside of her.

"I don't have to prove myself to you or anyone else. Now get out," Aislinn said quietly. This time when she turned, Baird let her go.

CHAPTER 7

*W*HAT THE HELL WAS THAT? Baird's mind was whirling with confusion and possibilities as he watched Aislinn walk to her shop. Part of him wanted to run after her and beg her to go out with him again. Watching her leave was harder than hearing what she had to say about herself.

His science mind scoffed at Aislinn's belief that she had some sort of power. And, yet, he'd just witnessed a small taste of it himself, hadn't he?

Baird began to clean up the table and examined his own feelings. Though he was shocked at what he had just discovered, he needed to decide if the news scared him or intrigued him.

Since he was already trying to figure out how it all worked, he supposed that it intrigued him, Baird thought.

Baird made a mental note to contact a few doctors that he knew in Dublin. They specialized in learning the intricacies of intuition. Perhaps they'd have some light to shine on this.

Baird checked his watch. He needed to unpack and get his things in order. Now would not be the time to go out to the cove, but before the week was over he'd make a point of venturing out to this much-talked-about beach.

Casting his gaze back on the shop, Baird forced himself to leave. It looked like he had some research to do.

CHAPTER 8

*A*ISLINN'S HANDS TREMBLED as she moved invoices around on her desk. She dropped a pencil and bent to get it, surprised that tears pricked her eyes.

Damn it. She was not going to cry over Baird. She barely knew the man.

Which is why you shouldn't have slept with him, her conscience lectured her.

Aislinn slammed her fist on the desk. More than anything, she hated how he made her feel – like she needed to check into the loony bin. Though she knew she had her moments of being irrational, Aislinn was quite certain she wasn't crazy.

With a sigh, she went to unlock the front door. Saturdays were typically busy as the tour buses brought through hordes of gift-seeking tourists. Bracing herself for the onslaught of people in her shop and all of the emotions that they brought with them, Aislinn examined her inventory. She was getting low on her hand-painted postcards and made a note to pick up more blank cards this week.

As if on cue, the bells above the door chimed a cheerful greeting and Aislinn turned to greet her first customer of the day, grateful for the distraction.

Hours later, Aislinn stretched and wandered back to her small kitchenette to freshen up her tea. One thing that was great about running her own business was that it didn't allow her a lot of time to sulk over personal problems. Pleased with the day's sales, Aislinn thought about closing the shop for a few days next week to focus on painting and printing more photographs for the shop. She did that occasionally – closed her store on a whim. She knew that it drove some people crazy, but Aislinn refused to let her business run her. As soon as she felt like a slave to her work, she'd leave it. Freedom to make her own decisions was vitally important to her.

The bells chimed again and Aislinn turned to smile at the new customer and stopped short.

A slim girl stood just within the door, examining a rack of small black-and-white photos that Aislinn had on display. Aislinn recognized her and had heard talk of the girl through the small town. Her name was Morgan and she'd recently signed on to work on Flynn's fishing boats. She couldn't have been more than nineteen years old and had a startling beauty that was only heightened by the softness of her youth. Aislinn was also a hundred percent certain that she was looking at another one of Grace O'Malley's descendants.

Instead of calling out her usual cheerful greeting, Aislinn stayed where she was and watched Morgan move through the room. She stopped dead at a photograph of the cove, shot at sunset when the rays of the sun pierced the entrance to the cove and played on the cliffs protecting the sandy beach. It was one of Aislinn's favorites and she wasn't surprised that Morgan had stopped to examine it.

The girl reached up to lift the picture and check the price. The painting slipped from her hand and Aislinn gasped as it stopped mid-fall, hovering briefly in the air before returning to the wall while Morgan's hands remained at her side.

Morgan whipped her head around at Aislinn's gasp and pierced her with her eyes.

"Sorry, I'll just be leaving," Morgan said brusquely and fled towards the door.

"Hold up," Aislinn shouted.

Morgan paused at the door, her hand on the knob.

"It's fine. You can touch my pictures," Aislinn said soothingly, glossing over what she had just seen. Morgan stayed with her back turned. With a shrug, she just nodded and looked down at her hand.

"Would you like to stay? Have a cup of tea?"

"No, I have to go," Morgan mumbled but she hesitated.

"Morgan. Stop. I know that you're one of us."

Morgan's head whipped around and a ripple of anger flashed across her face. Aislinn almost took an involuntary step back before she steadied herself.

"You don't know a damn thing about me," Morgan hissed.

"Oh really? I know that you can tell when someone is reading your mind. I saw how you acted when Cait tried to figure it out. And, try as you might, you can't hide your feelings from me, and I see a lost, scared, and very angry young woman. Now, you can either turn your back on one of the few people who actually understands you or you can get right on out of my shop. I have no time for people who refuse to accept what they are." Aislinn tried to center her breathing. She knew that she was taking some of her anger at Baird out on Morgan but she didn't care. It seemed to her like the girl needed a quick lesson in what was what.

Morgan's shoulders slumped and she took her hand off the doorknob.

"I'll have that tea, I guess," she whispered.

"Lock the door, I'm done for the day," Aislinn decided and went to put the teapot on the stove.

CHAPTER 9

*A*ISLINN STAYED SILENT as she gathered cups for tea and motioned to Morgan to step into her courtyard. Her mind raced as she thought about how to approach Morgan. Though she'd seen several instances of Grace O'Malley's power in action, she'd yet to see anyone move something through the air.

Telekinesis.

Fascinating, Aislinn thought and stepped into the sunny courtyard. Morgan sat at her picnic table, hunched over, and refused to meet her eyes.

"Oh stop with the pathetic act," Aislinn said, her patience done for the day, "I'm not going to attack you."

Morgan started and then a hint of a smile slid across her beautiful features.

"I've heard you're a character," Morgan said, her voice heavy and warm like whiskey, a voice that was too old – too seductive – for her age.

"Aye, I am at that." Aislinn shrugged off the hurt that could come with a statement like that. She'd long ago stopped worrying about whether people considered her an eccentric artist or just crazy.

"Thank you," Morgan said softly when Aislinn slid her a cup of tea. Aislinn eased herself onto the bench across from the girl and studied her in silence. Aislinn sensed an underlying strength that belied Morgan's whipcord frame. Dark hair hung almost to her waist and her eyes were a startling mix of blue and green…almost a sea green. Aislinn imagined that Morgan must have had her fair share of suitors. She wondered if Morgan and Patrick had ever hooked up. Patrick, the main bartender at Cait's pub, had nursed a crush on Morgan for a few months now. Aislinn had yet to see them out and about together though. In fact, Aislinn rarely saw Morgan, which made her wonder where she slept. She said as much.

"I sleep in my van, mainly," Morgan admitted and Aislinn gaped at her.

"Why?"

Morgan shrugged and stared down at her cup. "Apartments require too much information."

Aislinn gestured with her cup for Morgan to go on.

"You know, background checks, references, that type of stuff."

"Maybe in a big city, but not in a place like Grace's Cove. Does Flynn know where you are sleeping?" Knowing Flynn, Morgan's boss and Keelin's husband, she was certain he would be appalled at the thought of Morgan sleeping in her car.

"No! And you mustn't tell him," Morgan said fiercely, pride flashing across her face.

"Morgan, he would help you. Do you need more

money? Is that it?" Aislinn couldn't imagine that being an apprentice on a fishing boat paid much.

Morgan shrugged her shoulders and then gave a small nod.

"I'll hire you part-time," Aislinn said and almost kicked herself. Where had that come from?

A flash of shock and then a sliver of pure joy rippled across Morgan's face.

"You will?"

Aislinn sighed. That flash of hope – of happiness – had told Aislinn everything that she needed to know. There was no way that she could let Morgan suffer. They were relatives of a sort, after all.

"On one condition – you tell me everything," Aislinn said and watched Morgan carefully. Morgan stiffened and then stared down into her cup before beginning to rise.

"Thank you for the offer then, but I'll have to decline."

Aislinn threw up her hands. "Morgan, sit. I swear, save me from dramatic people…" Aislinn rolled her eyes and stared across the table at Morgan. "Just give me the basics of why you are here and where you came from. We'll talk about your power in a moment."

Morgan flinched at the mention of her power.

"Yes. I have power too. You aren't the only one, sista, so don't get up on your high horse about it."

Morgan huffed out a small laugh.

"Trust me, that's the one thing that I have little ego about."

"So? Talk to me, Morgan. If I don't know you, I won't trust you alone in my shop."

Morgan nodded at that and tucked her long hair behind her ear. "I suppose that makes sense."

Aislinn leaned back and crossed her arms over her chest, waiting for Morgan to go on.

"Well, I'm from Killarney. I just turned nineteen and have been on my own for a while. Too long, actually." Morgan shrugged her shoulder and dismissed the fact quickly. "I was raised in an orphanage. Every time I was given to a foster home, I was returned. Basically the nuns raised me off and on, between homes. I took off when I was sixteen and have pretty much been on the road since."

Aislinn's heart broke a bit for Morgan. Knowing how hard it was when her family split up, she couldn't imagine not having a family at all. It also didn't take much for Aislinn to connect the dots.

"Let me guess…those foster homes. They saw you use your power, didn't they? And they were scared of you?"

Morgan's eyes filled with tears – so suddenly that Aislinn almost jumped across the table. The empathic part of her could feel years of Morgan's pain and anguish at being different come bubbling to the surface.

"Yes, they always returned me. The nuns…the nuns used to tell me that the devil was in me. They even tried to perform an exorcism on me."

Aislinn stared at the girl in horror. She wanted to go across the table, hug Morgan, and tell her that everything was going to be okay. But Aislinn's instincts told her that Morgan would bolt if she did.

"Well, that was right stupid of them, wasn't it?" Aislinn said casually and was rewarded with a small smile from Morgan.

"Aye, it was at that," Morgan agreed.

"So, you haven't really had anyone to tell you what you are or how you got to be this way, have you?" Aislinn asked.

"No, I did some research though and that is how I landed in Grace's Cove. I figured if I could get on a fishing vessel maybe I could get into the cove from another angle and figure some things out."

"It's tough to grow up with power. It must be even harder not to have anyone to explain it to you."

"Did you? Did your mom explain it?" Morgan asked.

"Ah, well, yes, she did. Luckily, we moved back to Grace's Cove when I was a teenager and I was able to meet Fiona. She had a larger impact on me than my mother ever did."

"The healer?"

"Aye, I'll take you to meet her."

"I…I think that I'd like that," Morgan said hesitantly. She twisted a piece of hair through her fingers.

"Here's the deal, Morgan…if you come into this, want to be a part of us, then you're in it. You get me? Keelin, Cait, Fiona…we are all, in an odd way, connected and family. I know that you don't have family, but we would be it. So, you have to decide if you are ready for that. If you are used to being on your own…it could be hard for you to understand that." Aislinn picked her words carefully, wanting to show Morgan that she could have a family but not scare the girl by insisting that she become friends with everyone.

"I…I'd have to think about it to be honest. I'd like to work for you. Your shop is beautiful, it would be an honor.

I'm not sure if I am ready for the rest yet," Morgan said softly.

"I understand. But you have to promise me one thing – no hiding and no lying. That's one of the benefits of my ability – I can tell if you lie to me."

Morgan nodded.

"I promise. No lying. Despite everything or maybe because of it, I'm an exceptionally loyal person."

Aislinn could tell that she spoke the truth.

"You'll need to meet Fiona. Not right away, but…she's just amazing. She took all of us in and taught us about ourselves. She's become like a grandmother to me."

Morgan smiled. "That sounds nice. Having someone like that in my life."

"Let me show you around the shop and then I'll call Shane. I bet he'll be able to hook you up with an affordable apartment, okay?"

Morgan nodded her head eagerly and for the first time, Aislinn saw a wide, unencumbered smile light up the girl's face. Aislinn almost gasped. When the worry dropped away from Morgan's face, she was stunning. Making a note to draw her sometime, Aislinn led the way back into the shop.

CHAPTER 10

*T*HE NEXT MORNING Aislinn sat at a chair in the back corner of her courtyard and sipped a cup of tea while she idly sketched Morgan from memory. The girl had opened up when she had shown her around the shop and Aislinn could tell that she was truly excited about the opportunity. She'd have to think about how she could get Morgan up to Fiona's.

"Yoohoo! Darling!"

Aislinn dropped her pencil as her mother's voice called to her over the fence.

"Mum! I wasn't expecting you," Aislinn said as she rose to cross the courtyard. In a moment she was enveloped in a warm hug and the scent of Chanel No. 5. Pulling back, she studied her mother's face.

Mary was the spitting image of Aislinn. Her face was interesting, unusual, worldly even. Unlike Aislinn, she had cropped her curls to chin length and they rioted around her face in a dusky shade of deep auburn. Several colorful scarves were wound around her neck and Mary's wrists jangled with a mass amount of mismatched bracelets. Her mother was all energy and life and she created a disturbance wherever she went.

Mary's eyes narrowed as she took in Aislinn's face and shadowed eyes.

"What's wrong? Tell me immediately," Mary demanded.

Aislinn sighed. They were too closely linked for her to hide anything from her mother. Though Mary's ability ran more to foretelling the future, she was always on point when her daughter was upset.

"Come in, let's sit," Aislinn said and gestured to her table.

Mary surveyed the courtyard and sniffed.

"Let's go somewhere fun for lunch. Is Flynn's restaurant open for lunch on the weekends?"

Resigned, Aislinn nodded. That meant she'd have to go put makeup on, and she counted to three in her head.

"Why don't you go put some makeup on and get ready? My treat," Mary said and smiled brightly at her daughter.

Aislinn laughed at her and bent to kiss her cheek. Her mother never changed. Always look your best, have fun at everything you do, and be open to meeting new people was Mary's motto. Once Mary had left Sean, it was like her mother had blossomed.

In her bedroom, Aislinn changed into a turquoise top and skinny jeans. She clipped her curls half-back and added some dangly earrings that she had just made. Pulling out her concealer, she covered the dark shadows that bruised her eyes and put a light dusting of eye shadow on.

Slicking on some lip gloss, she grabbed her purse and met her mom down in the shop.

"There, much better. You're such a pretty girl," Mary said, pride lacing her voice.

"Good genes," Aislinn said and smiled at her mom.

"Do you want to call Colin?" Mary asked. Colin and Mary's relationship was still strained even though Mary popped into Grace's Cove a few times a month to visit him and her grandson, Finn.

"No, let's just do us girls," Aislinn said, not in the mood for a serving of family tension with lunch.

Mary looped her arm through Aislinn's as they left the shop and walked down the hill towards the harbor. Colorful shops toppled on top of each other down the street and the effect was charming and inviting. Aislinn loved walking through the streets and admiring the eclectic mix of galleries, pottery studios, music shops, and other novelty stores. The tourists loved the charm of the small town, and the brightly painted buildings made a perfect backdrop for vacation pictures.

The street ended in a T at the harbor. Flynn's restaurant, a nondescript building with a nautical design, sat close to the water and Aislinn could almost taste his famous mussels from the scents that wafted their way.

"God, it never gets old, does it?" Mary said in reference to the mouthwatering smells that emanated from Flynn's restaurant.

"Not in the slightest," Aislinn agreed and held the door for her mother.

As Mary breezed past her to go into the restaurant, Aislinn turned to look at Baird's building half a block away. She gasped as she saw him standing in the large picture window on the second floor. Though they were too far apart for her to see his face, she could swear that his eyes bored into hers. Moving quickly into the restaurant, she shook off an involuntary shiver that ran through her.

Aislinn smiled as the waitress sat them. The restaurant was charming and simple, whitewashed stucco with fishing nets hanging on the walls. A chunky candle sputtered in the middle of the table and the windows were thrown open to catch the breeze off the water. Mary smiled and ordered a glass of white wine. She raised an eyebrow at Aislinn but Aislinn shook her head and ordered an iced tea.

"Darling, tell me what's wrong. Is it the man in the window?"

Aislinn laughed. Her mother hadn't even seen Baird and yet she still knew.

"You never cease to amaze me."

"Nor do you, my sweet girl. Tell me what's going on."

The waiter appeared to take their order, which gave Aislinn a few minutes to consider her words. They both ordered the mussels in the cilantro cream sauce. Mary waited patiently until the waiter left.

"I've met someone."

"Aha! The man in the window. Details!" Mary smiled exuberantly at her daughter and Aislinn had to laugh. Sometimes it was like they were girlfriends and not mother and daughter. She supposed that it had to do with the divorce as well as their shared mystical ability. Both of those things had drawn them closer together.

Aislinn looked around and kept her voice low. Small

towns were notorious for their gossip and Grace's Cove was no different.

"His name is Baird. He's thirty-three and works as a psychiatrist. He moved his practice down from Galway and wants to spend some time here. Says he was inexplicably drawn here."

Mary's eyes narrowed but she said nothing, motioning for Aislinn to go on.

"He came into my shop and I swear it was like I couldn't even see him! His aura radiated around him and it was like I got punched in the gut. I was totally flustered and awkward. I was certain that he would think that I was ridiculous and instead he asked to have a drink with me."

"Ah, a man who is direct. I like that," Mary said.

They paused as the waiter brought them their drinks. Aislinn took a sip of the cool tea and tried to center her thoughts.

"Yes. He's very direct. And analytical. Long story short...I sent him on his way," Aislinn said, glossing over their night of shared passion.

"Hmm, I imagine that there is quite a bit you aren't telling me. Which is fine!" Mary raised her hand in a stop motion to Aislinn. "Mothers don't need to know every detail to surmise what is going on."

Aislinn smiled at her mother.

"Why did you send him on his way, honey? What happened?"

"I...well, I guess it was a couple things."

Aislinn waited as their lunch was served. She sighed in pure bliss at the first bite and allowed the rich flavors to melt on her tongue. Mary moaned her appreciation from across the table.

"Best mussels in the country, hands down."

"Mum, can I ask you a question?"

Mary made a go-ahead gesture with her fork.

"Why did you leave Da? I know of most of the reasons…but I've always felt it was because you were so different. Was that it?"

"That was a huge part of it. Obviously you know about Margaret as you are friends with Keelin now. Even I knew about Margaret when your father and I first started dating. But, for some reason I felt like I could fix him – like I could fill that hole in his heart. And, we were good, for a while. But soon the novelty of trying to fix him grew old and our differences became more apparent. He's a fine man…just not for me. I would have left him far earlier if it wasn't for you and Colin."

Aislinn hung her head as the old guilt swept through her. "I know."

"Oh, stop. It's not your fault. I just needed you to be old enough to understand what was going on is all."

"I did understand. That didn't make it any easier."

"I know, sweetheart. I know. But sometimes in life you have to follow your heart. Your father and I continuing to be miserable would have done nothing for you both."

Aislinn nodded and picked at her food silently.

"Is that what you're worried about with this Baird? That you like him too much and it will end horribly?" Mary asked.

"Well, that's one element of it. We are just too differ-ent. Though my attraction to him was immediate and

visceral, he's an uptight, analytical doctor…and I'm me."
Aislinn shrugged her shoulders helplessly. "The man wears
wire-framed glasses for God's sake!"

Mary laughed at her and took a long sip of her wine.
They sat in silence for a moment and Aislinn waited for
the typical Mary response – go on and have fun, girl!

"I think that you are probably right," Mary finally said.

"What?" Aislinn leaned back in surprise.

"I hate to say this, but yes, you may be too different. If
you can't find a common ground of similarity, it may be
too hard to hold onto the relationship. I know that they say
opposites attract but I've only ever seen those types of relationships work when there is a healthy balance."

Aislinn considered her words carefully. "So, if I find
no common ground…run?"

"Maybe, yes."

Aislinn sighed and stirred her mussels around in the
cream sauce, picking at the shells.

"He thinks I'm crazy."

"Well, we are a little out there, Aislinn."

"No, I mean like really crazy. I told him about my
ability and he told me that he believed that *I* believe that I
have power. Which in shrink talk means he thinks that I
am nuts."

Mary leaned back and crossed her arms across her
chest and sniffed.

"Well, I never. How could he say such a thing? What
with you running a successful business and creating beautiful art? No crazy person would be able to hold down
something like that!" Mary's words were indignant and
Aislinn smiled at her.

"Thanks, Mom."

"Speaking of your art, I ran into the loveliest man in Dublin last week. He's the curator for one of the major galleries. I told him about your work and he asked me to send some pictures of it…maybe set up a show. What do you think?"

Aislinn's mouth dropped open and a mixture of panic and excitement raced through her.

"Mum! That's wonderful news. Do you think that my work is good enough?"

Mary gave her a derisive glance. "Do I think your work is good enough? Please. Your work is outstanding. I brag about you all over Ireland. I hand out your cards constantly. I couldn't be prouder of you."

Tears pricked Aislinn's eyes, surprising her.

"Thanks, Mum."

Mary reached across the table and patted Aislinn's hand.

"Don't let that Baird get to you, honey. It sounds like you walk two different paths. I would stay far away from him."

CHAPTER 11

*B*AIRD WATCHED THE two women enter Flynn's restaurant. The other woman could only be Aislinn's mother as the resemblance was uncanny. He sighed and turned away from the window, running his hand through his thick hair.

He already missed her.

Shaking his head, Baird snagged his coffee cup from the counter and went to sit in front of his streamlined laptop. He'd spent much of the night researching different disorders where people thought they had otherworldly powers. Late into the night, he'd finally succumbed to his curiosity and had started researching intuition and empathic abilities.

The research had proved to be fascinating and hours later, Baird had made the decision to contact a few colleagues that conducted research on intuitive abilities in Dublin. He'd dashed off a quick email with a few questions and hoped to see a response today.

As if on cue, his email indicated new mail. Taking a sip of coffee, he opened the mail and perused the contents.

"Really…" Baird said.

It shouldn't have surprised him. As someone who studied the human brain he was well aware that there was still much to be discovered about its power.

His colleagues had sent him pages of research studies documenting various intuitive abilities along with scientific explanations for the reasoning behind them. They also expressed great interest in meeting his "friend" and helping her to understand where her ability came from. Baird wondered if Aislinn would be interested in talking to psychiatrists and scientists about herself. Though she'd been open with him about it, a part of him suspected she would spit in his face if he asked.

Baird leaned back in the chair and ran his hands over his face. He couldn't stop thinking about her. Her scent, the softness of her skin under his touch, the way her smile changed her face from interesting to beautiful. He wanted to be with her…laughing with her…watching her work.

Was he scared of her? Of her powers? Or did he think she was a nutter? Baird couldn't quite convince himself that Aislinn was crazy, which left him with the distinctly uneasy feeling that he would have to accept her as she was if he wanted to be with her.

Baird pulled out his map of the village of Grace's Cove. In order to understand all of this, it looked like he needed to go to the source. Examining the map, he made plans to head to the cove the next day.

CHAPTER 12

I WOULD STAY FAR *away from him.* Mary's words echoed in Aislinn's head the next morning. Though her head agreed with her mother, her heart seemed to be of a different mind.

Traitor, she whispered down to her heart and went to gather her art supplies. She had decided to take the day off and go out of the village to paint the cove. Her mother had come back to the shop yesterday and taken pictures of all of her work. Mary had said that the gallery was looking to feature seascapes and Aislinn knew of few places more stunning than the rocky cliffs that hugged the mystical waters of the cove.

Aislinn decided that she would pop in on Fiona and put a word in her ear about Morgan and then head down to the cliffs to paint.

Aislinn went out to load her battered station wagon with her art supplies. Mary sneered at Aislinn's choice of vehicles, but Aislinn secretly loved it. It was serviceable, her easel and paint supplies fit nicely in the back, and she never worried about the wagon getting scraped up on rough roads. Aislinn sniffed. Baird probably drove a fancy sedan that was pristine inside, with one of those little bags for any snippets of rubbish.

Further convincing herself that they were far too different to be in a relationship, Aislinn pushed Baird from her mind and took the sea road out to Fiona's cottage in the hills. With the windows rolled down to encourage the sea breeze, Aislinn expertly maneuvered the one-lane road that hugged the cliffs. Sunlight cut through puffy clouds that hung over water that seemed a little restless today. Perfect, Aislinn thought. Moody water and sunlight poking through clouds always made for interesting paintings. Aislinn loved to play with light and mood. It showed in her seascapes and allowed her to command a high price for her work.

Aislinn turned at a hook in the road and bumped up the lane towards Fiona's cottage. Aside from her mother, Fiona was the most important woman in Aislinn's life and she had played a major role in helping Aislinn to navigate the murky waters of being a teenager with an extra-special gift. Aislinn credited Fiona with steering her from trouble and keeping her on the path of art. In doing so, she'd freed Aislinn from any expectations other than to be herself and had given her the true gift of happiness and confidence in her path in life.

Aislinn smiled at the weathered cottage as she approached it. She always felt good when she came here and even more so now that Ronan was staying with Fiona. Ronan, an Irish setter, was a gift to Keelin from Flynn. Yet, lately, Ronan had been sticking around with Fiona. A cottage out in the wild needed a good dog for protection, Aislinn thought, and smiled when Ronan came bounding around the corner at the sound of a car.

"Ah, there's the ferocious beast himself." Aislinn called to Ronan and he barked up at her, his tail wagging. Pulling the wagon to a stop, Aislinn bounded out of the car and sunk to her knees to wrap her arms around Ronan's wiggling body. He lapped her face with his rough tongue and breaking away, ran to grab a stick.

"Aye, it's a game of fetch you'll be wanting then, is it?" Aislinn laughed at Ronan and tossed the stick. He bounded exuberantly through the green field that surrounded Fiona's cottage. Aislinn turned to survey the cottage. It looked like Flynn was keeping up on any repairs needed and Fiona's window boxes bloomed with a happy bunch of flowers. The gray stone cottage mixed perfectly with the surrounding landscape and the view was worth millions, Aislinn thought as she turned to survey the wide expanse of meadow that dropped off into cliffs that soared over the ocean.

"Ash, dear! What a surprise," Fiona's warm voice called to her from around the corner of the house.

Aislinn detoured from her path to the front door and around the cottage to the garden that Fiona carefully tended behind the cottage. The old woman wore khaki pants, a men's-style shirt and a large straw hat to shade her from the sun. Her eyes were sharp with intelligence and her face creased with a welcoming smile. Aislinn instantly felt at peace, just watching her gather her herbs in small baskets. Fiona had always had that effect on her. She was the port in Aislinn's storm.

Careful not to stomp on any of Fiona's plants, Aislinn stepped to Fiona and bent to give her a lingering hug. Pulling back, Fiona eyed Aislinn's face carefully.

"Hmm, let's take a break. I just made some sun tea this morning. We can sit at the table out here."

"Sounds lovely," Aislinn said. "Do you need help?"

"No, please. Just throw the stick for Ronan. He needs a playmate."

"Where's Teagan?"

Fiona shrugged her shoulders. "Who knows with that dog? She comes and goes as she pleases. Fickle woman," Fiona laughed and went into the cottage.

Aislinn sat at the small table and chairs that were positioned best to capture the sun without sacrificing a view of the cove. She thought about how Fiona had known who was visiting her without even stepping around the cottage. Aislinn wanted to discuss Morgan with her. Fiona seemed to have a touch of all of the powers…though her healing power was the most powerful. Yet, to Aislinn's knowledge, she'd never seen Fiona move something without her hands.

"Here we go," Fiona said as she turned the corner of the cottage with a tray full of tea, scones, and a small plate of fruit.

"This is lovely, thank you," Aislinn said and reached for her glass as Fiona settled into the chair next to her. They both watched as Ronan raced across the field after a stick, tumbling over himself in his excitement.

"He brings me such joy," Fiona laughed.

"I know. I've thought about getting a dog. Maybe a cat, instead. I don't know if I am responsible enough for a dog," Aislinn said.

Fiona leveled her eyes at Aislinn. "Yes, I suppose that you would chafe at the restriction that a dog places on you. You've built yourself a nice little world where you can come and go as you please, haven't you?"

Aislinn shrugged against the perceived sting in Fiona's words. "Is that a bad thing?"

"I didn't say that it was. I just know that being tied down to something for too long, aside from your business, is hard for you."

Aislinn shrugged and studied the line of where the water met the sky.

"Things can change quickly. It's easier to be flexible and able to adapt to change, in my mind," Aislinn said.

Fiona only nodded, not saying anything.

Aislinn sighed. "Okay, I know that when you stay silent you are trying to get me to talk. You can't pull that on me anymore."

Fiona only smiled and raised an eyebrow at her.

Aislinn threw her hands up.

"Yes, I met a man. And, yes, I don't do attachments well. Okay, happy?" Aislinn huffed out a breath and crossed her arms across her chest.

Fiona let out a lusty laugh that had Aislinn cracking her own smile.

"Ah, Ash, you've always been one of my favorites."

"Really? Thanks," Aislinn said in surprise.

"Really. You have such talent and such self-confidence…and yet you keep yourself aloof from others. Never vulnerable. In doing so, you make it difficult to be in relationships with others."

"I don't know if I agree with that!" Aislinn said heatedly. "I told Baird about my gift. I was honest! Do you know how hard it is to tell someone that – knowing that they will judge you?"

"Baird? Hmm, so it's the new doctor in town. I've heard talk of him. A handsome one, no?"

Aislinn sighed and dug the toe of her hiking shoes into the ground. "Yes, tall, dark, and yum as Cait calls him. He even has these wire-framed glasses…"

"Well, if he has glasses, then I'm sunk too," Fiona agreed.

Aislinn flashed a small smile at Fiona before taking a sip of her cool tea.

"He thinks that I'm a nutter. That I just *believe* that I have this magickal power but that I don't really. I even proved it to him. Which…I've never done before. I've never felt like I've had to prove myself to anyone. Which makes me furious, to be honest," Aislinn said quietly.

"Ah, a skeptic. I suppose that makes sense with the business that he is in."

"Yes, but he didn't try to stop me. Didn't try to understand more. He just let me walk. So, I suppose that's my answer." Aislinn shrugged her shoulders and stared moodily at the sea.

"Is it?"

"Well? I'm not going to hunt him down and keep trying to explain who I am to him. It wouldn't matter anyway. We're simply too different."

"Ah, well, then I guess that is all there is to say about that," Fiona said demurely.

Aislinn rolled her eyes. "I'm used to your tactics, old woman, and you aren't making me talk any more about this. I've already talked to my mum about this and she agrees that I need to stay far away."

"Not surprising," Fiona said.

"And, I have something more interesting to discuss. Have you met Morgan?"

Fiona smiled at Aislinn's change of subject but let it pass.

"I saw her at Keelin's wedding. Beautiful girl. Touch of something...I haven't figured out what as of yet. She's fairly elusive. Flynn says she is a hard worker but keeps to herself and doesn't talk much."

Aislinn should have known that Fiona would have all the pertinent details.

"That touch of something? It's telekinesis."

Fiona's mouth dropped open and Aislinn felt a sliver of delight sneak through her. There was very little that got past Fiona and it was rare to see her react in surprise. Giving herself a mental high five, she smiled at Fiona.

"No!"

"Yes, indeed. I saw it for myself or I wouldn't have believed it."

"I've never heard of this particular manifestation of Grace's blood. Let me get my book."

Fiona hurried away to get her book and Aislinn bent to scratch Ronan's ears. At the very least, the change of subject had taken the focus off of Aislinn's relationship with Baird. Her non-relationship, she reminded herself.

Fiona hurried around the corner with a small book. Its beauty was in its simplicity. Aged leather, softened at the creases, wrapped around vellum pages. Aislinn knew that it was Grace O'Malley's book of healing potions but she suspected that there was other information within the pages that she knew little of.

Aislinn stayed silent as Fiona flipped through the book and murmured to herself.

"Ah, hmm. Here we may have something." Fiona finally spoke.

She handed the book to Aislinn, who took it carefully. The pages were delicate and should have been handled with gloves on, but Aislinn was used to touching delicate works. She held the book gently by the leather and examined the passage that Fiona had pointed to.

'Tis by the moon and the stars,

A fleeting movement,

A special touch of magick,

One that with the mind does feel,

As though one may lift without the physical body,

A dash of fae,

Only those who need it most,

Will be gifted this touch.

"To those who need it most..." Aislinn repeated.

"What do you know of Morgan's background?" Fiona asked as Aislinn handed the book back.

"I'm hiring her for the shop. So, what I tell you is in confidence."

"Understood and good for you. You've a good heart."

"She's an orphan. Essentially raised by nuns as her foster families would return her after they saw her ability. She's angry. Very angry and very lonely."

Fiona nodded.

"You'll bring her to me?"

"If I can get her to come. Otherwise you'll have to come to the shop. I'm trying to get her a place to stay as she is sleeping in her van."

"Shane will help. I'll make him."

"Already taken care of." Aislinn smiled at Fiona and stood. "I'm off to paint while the light is good. Mum has a potential offer for a show lined up for me in Dublin and I'll need new inventory."

"Wonderful! I'm so proud of you. Such talent," Fiona said and stood to wrap her arms around Aislinn. "Now, don't forget to listen to your heart, young one…"

"We'll see," Aislinn called over her shoulder as she got in her wagon.

CHAPTER 13

*A*ISLINN DROVE FURTHER down the lane from Fiona's cottage and pulled her car to the side of the road behind a long line of bushes. Getting out, she assessed which angle she wanted to paint the cove from. If she painted from the road, she wouldn't be able to capture the sheer magnitude of the cliffs that jutted out into the sea. Instead, she decided to cut across the fields to set up her easel by a pile of rocky outcroppings. The rocks would shelter her from the wind and allow her some privacy in her painting.

Aislinn pulled her small, transportable easel out of the back of the wagon along with her art supplies and set out across the field. The mid-afternoon light was lovely and would soften as the day wore on.

Aislinn set up her easel behind the rocks and pulled out her small collapsible stool that allowed her to sit at the same level as her canvas. Considering her supplies for a moment, she pulled out her oils. Though she loved to work in watercolor, Aislinn was feeling moody. The richness of oils would allow her a more dramatic contrast in her painting. Preparing the canvas for painting, Aislinn began laying the gesso on the canvas, outlining the starkness of the cliffs against the sea.

Humming to herself, she allowed herself to go into an almost trancelike state. Aislinn rarely spoke of her creative process. She wouldn't know how to explain it if she tried. Part of being empathic meant that she could feel other people's feelings. What most people didn't know or understand was that it went far deeper than that. To Aislinn, everything had its own unique energy and aura. Plants glowed to her, water churned with its own vibration, and light tingled. It all had feeling and movement to her. When Aislinn painted, the world fell away and simply pulsed in color and feelings. That was what Aislinn painted…not what most people saw. She supposed that was why people connected so viscerally with her art. Her paintings captured the feelings of the natural world that most people were unable to identify or express for themselves.

Something broke into her zone and she tried to swat it away as she concentrated on her canvas. Again, a disturbance. Cursing, she forced herself to look away from the canvas and to stare at the cove. What had broken her concentration?

"Aw, shit," Aislinn cursed furiously as she saw Baird's head bob along the field before disappearing from sight on the path into the cove.

"Of course he would go there. Of course he would! Does that man have no sense?" Aislinn cursed steadily as she rose from her stool. In a flat-out run, she raced across the meadow, the ground soft beneath her boots.

Aislinn stumbled to a stop at the top of the ledge leading to the beach below her. The cove was an almost perfect half-circle, its cliffs reaching high into the air and protecting the long stretch of sand that lay at the bottom of their rocky walls. A narrow path switchbacked down the sheer face of the cliff wall and spilled out onto the beach. Aislinn could just make out Baird at the bottom.

"Baird! Wait! Baird, don't go on the beach!" Aislinn shouted but her words were carried away on the wind. On an oath, she raced down the path, trailing her hand along the rocky wall to keep herself balanced. Her breath came in ragged gasps and she struggled to tamp down on the panic that rose in her throat. Baird stepped onto the sand and Aislinn's heart stopped just for a moment.

"Baird, no!" Aislinn screeched and this time, he heard.

Baird turned at the sound of her voice and looked up at her in confusion. Aislinn watched in horror as a wave gathered strength and rose high behind Baird.

"No!" Aislinn screamed right before the wave crashed over Baird, taking him under with it.

CHAPTER 14

*A*ISLINN SCRAMBLED THE rest of the way along the
path and raced out onto the beach.

"Shit, shit, shit." She stopped and drew a circle around
herself, patting herself hysterically until her hand grazed
over a bracelet that she had made recently.

"I come here in peace. We come here in peace. Please
don't harm him. He doesn't know about any of this. I
promise that we are here for nothing but the purest of
purposes. We respect you," Aislinn gasped out as she
heaved her bracelet into the water. Without hesitation she
ran towards where Baird's crumpled form lay on the sand.
The wave had tossed him across the sand several times and
another one had hit him for good measure. Please let him
be okay, she prayed.

Kneeling by his side, Aislinn grabbed at his wet arms,
trying to turn him over. Baird moaned and moved at her
touch and Aislinn let out a breath that she hadn't realized
she'd been holding.

"Baird…Baird, it's me, Aislinn. Turn over if you can,"

Aislinn whispered urgently. Baird rolled and looked up at her, a dazed look in his eyes, blood running down his face from beneath his hair.

"Oh no, oh. Shit, Baird, this may seem weird but... give me something." Aislinn scanned his body and the only thing that she could see on him that was an option was his glasses or his belt. How his glasses had stayed on his face during that fall was beyond her, but Aislinn didn't have time to wonder. "Give me your belt."

"What? Aislinn?"

There was no time to waste. Aislinn reached for his belt buckle and undid the clasp quickly before pulling it from his pants. Baird lifted his back grudgingly so she could slip it from under him and silently watched her.

Aislinn stood and traced a circle in the sand around Baird. For good measure, she leaned over and swiped a bit of blood from his face and rubbed it into his belt.

"Say what I say," Aislinn ordered. "I mean the cove no harm."

"I mean the cove no harm," Baird whispered.

"My purpose for being here is pure. I respect these sacred waters."

"My purpose for being here is pure. I respect these sacred waters."

Aislinn threw the belt into the water and watched as it landed with a plop. A small wave seemed to reach up and swallow it whole and Aislinn shivered. Feeling safer, she knelt by Baird's head.

"Let me look at your head," Aislinn said and bent over him, her face close to his.

"What happened? How did that happen? I was so far

from the water," Baird said in confusion. Anger whipped across his face and he struggled to rise. Aislinn pushed him back down on the sand.

"Just rest, I'll explain. I need to look at your cut."

Aislinn pushed his thick hair aside until she could see where the blood was coming from. A small cut, no more than a thumbnail's width, bled with a ferocity that belied its small stature.

"You've a cut up here. Small, but deep. I doubt you'll need stitches though. We should get a compress on it. Do you have a hankie?"

Baird reached into his pocket and pulled out a crisp linen square, now soaking wet. Aislinn rolled her eyes. *Of course* he would have a handkerchief.

Aislinn folded the square of linen and first wiped Baird's face before pressing the cloth to his cut. Baird winced slightly and then met her eyes. Their faces were mere inches apart and Aislinn felt a warm tug low in her belly.

"Is this why people won't come here? Freak waves?"

Aislinn sighed and blew out a breath, concentrating on keeping pressure on his head. Baird reached up and pushed her hand away to hold the cloth himself.

"Why don't we get out of the water?" Aislinn gestured to an area of sand by a small rocky outcropping.

Baird nodded and Aislinn helped him to rise. Together they walked silently across the sand until they reached the outcropping. They both eased onto the warm sand and leaned against the rocks, shoulder to shoulder. The sun hung lower in the sky and its light pierced the opening of the cove to dance over them and the cliff walls that rose behind them. The placid water of the cove seemed to laugh at them.

Baird gestured to the water.

"Look at that. Calm as can be. What happened?'

Aislinn thought about how to answer him. Knowing that she was dealing with a science-minded person, she decided to go with the facts.

"The cove is enchanted."

Baird huffed out a laugh and shook his head.

"No way."

"Way. Very much way. This is Grace O'Malley's final resting place." Aislinn gestured to the calm waters. "She knew she was dying. Her daughter came with her. Together they enchanted the cove and Grace then walked into the water. Her daughter gave birth that very night on this beach. Powerful magick."

Baird remained silent and Aislinn gave him some time to mull that over.

"So, you're saying that Ireland's famous pirate queen had magickal powers?"

"Correct."

"I'm having a hard time believing that."

Aislinn smiled and looked out at the water. "It doesn't matter whether you believe it. It's the truth one way or the other."

"I'm sure that you believe that."

Aislinn felt a ripple of anger go through her. She noticed that the waves began to pick up and she waved her hand at them. "Would you knock that off? First, I don't suggest making me angry down here and second, I'm not crazy. I don't know how else you need proof that this is real. Apparently having the cove damn near kick your arse isn't enough for you."

"Is that what that was? The cove was mad at me?"

"Well? Do you think that I did that little protection ritual just for fun?"

"How do I know that it isn't you who made the wave come up?"

Aislinn jumped to her feet, sincerely offended. "How could you think that of me? That I would want to hurt you like that? I was trying to stop you from going into the cove!" Aislinn turned to leave him and Baird reared up to grab her arm. With one yank, he pulled her back down to the sand...half on top of him. Aislinn met his eyes, her anger and hurt apparent on her face.

"I'm sorry. You're right. I'm just so confused," Baird admitted gently.

"I would never hurt another human being. I have too much respect for life," Aislinn said stiffly.

"Aye, that was rude of me to say, I apologize again," Baird said. Aislinn lost herself for a moment, staring into eyes that seemed able to hypnotize her.

"Why did you throw my belt in the water?"

Aislinn cleared her throat and tried not to laugh. She must've seemed like a crazy woman. She hadn't been entirely sure if her first offering would cover Baird so she needed to make sure that he was protected.

"Just trying to get in your pants, sailor." Aislinn leered at him.

"Good, because that's all that I can think about myself," Baird said and rolled on top of her.

Aislinn gasped as his hard body covered hers, pressing her back into the warm sand.

Baird didn't give Aislinn time to think. He nipped at her bottom lip and when she opened her mouth in a soft moan, he slipped his tongue between her lips. Aislinn jerked against his mouth, pushing his shoulders away with her hands. Baird moved his body sensually against hers and Aislinn felt heat flash through her. His lips were soothing her fears and arousing her at the same time.

All the lines seemed to blur in her head and Aislinn allowed herself simply to feel. As his warmth washed over her, she wrapped her arms around his neck and pulled him closer in invitation. Baird moaned against her mouth and moved his lips down her neck to the sensitive spot at the nape. Aislinn shivered against his lips.

"I can't get you out of my head. I can't think straight," Baird whispered at her throat and Aislinn found herself nodding helplessly against his shoulder.

"Aye, I don't know what to believe with you. Or how to believe in this. But I believe in us. And maybe that's enough," Baird said and kissed her again.

Baird's words tumbled in her head. Was it enough? Did he have to believe or understand everything about her? Aislinn felt like there was a fine line that she was missing there but lost her train of thought as Baird slipped a hand beneath the tank that she wore and found her breast. Aislinn moaned into his mouth and arched her back as he expertly toyed with her nipple, sending sensations straight to her core. She squirmed against Baird, pushing her legs open so the length of him rested between her legs.

Aislinn ground herself against his hardness, craving

contact. Baird continued to torture her breasts with his hands. On a soft curse, he reached to the waistband of her jeans and unzipped them. Aislinn moved to take them off but he stopped her.

"Let me," Baird said gently.

Leaning over, he brushed a kiss softly over her lips before slipping a hand beneath her underwear to find her slick and ready. Baird gave Aislinn a wicked smile that almost had her convulsing around his hand.

In one smooth movement, he slipped his fingers deep inside of her. Aislinn's hips bucked involuntarily against the intrusion and Baird laughed down at her – a master in his seduction – pulling her under much like the wave that had swallowed him earlier. In one expert movement, Baird drove her to the brink of ecstasy and as she convulsed around his hand, he captured her lips in a heated kiss.

Baird withdrew his hand and buttoned her pants. Aislinn eyed him curiously. On a sigh, he positioned his arms around her head and looked down at her.

"I want more than this. This is the easy part for us. This is as far as it can go. And, the light is getting low," Baird said.

Aislinn nodded. Everything he said made sense. Was sensible. But…she wanted more. She had to bring herself back from the emotions and auras that had enveloped her and try to be pragmatic.

"I understand. Um, thanks?" Aislinn said and Baird broke out in laughter.

"Anytime, doll," Baird said and stood up. Reaching down, he pulled her up from the sand and wrapped his arms around her. Aislinn allowed him to hold her for a moment, her head nestled against his chest. She watched the water of the cove and her heart skipped a beat as light shot from the bottom of the cove, illuminating the water in a deep blue color.

"What the hell is that?" Baird pulled her more tightly against him though his voice remained calm. He was protecting her, Aislinn thought dizzily.

"Um, nothing. Really. It just does that sometimes. Enchanted, remember?"

"I think we need to leave," Baird whispered.

"I couldn't agree more," Aislinn said. Together they raced across the sand to the path. Baird kept her hand in his and helped her to navigate the path up the cliff wall. Aislinn stayed silent on the trek, refusing to believe what she had just seen, what the cove was trying to tell her.

And that the cove never lied.

CHAPTER 15

*A*ISLINN WALKED WITH Baird across the field to the lane where he had parked his car. A late model sedan, Aislinn noted with a mental eye roll.

"How did you get here?" Baird asked, looking around the field.

Aislinn pointed to the line of bushes up the lane. "My car's up here. I was out painting along the ledge over there when I saw you go into the cove."

"And you came to save me," Baird said softly.

"Aye, I did. You clearly didn't know the ways of the cove or you wouldn't have gone down there on your own. I thought that you were smarter than that." Aislinn glared at him.

"Hey, my research didn't bring up anything like what just happened. The best that I could find was that people stayed away because they couldn't swim there due to a rough current."

Aislinn slapped her head. "Do you see how beautiful that beach is? Do you think that people would stay away from the beach if the only reason was that they couldn't go for a swim? Plenty of people spend time on beaches without swimming."

"Well, I didn't know the rest, did I? And, as I'm not one who's inclined to believe in magickal powers, how would I think to assume more?" Baird asked indignantly.

"I don't know how many more examples you need to see before you believe," Aislinn said wearily.

"Well, honestly, probably a lot more. Much of this…" Baird waved his hand, "could be an aberration."

Aislinn's mouth dropped open. An aberration? That was how he was going to explain it away? Aislinn just shook her head at him.

"What? Aislinn, listen, I really do want to be with you. I think about you constantly. But, I guess that I need some time to understand some of this." Baird waved his hand again.

"Well, take all the time you want in trying to understand it. As there's no answer to what simply is, you'll never understand it. I don't understand. None of us do. You either accept what is in front of your eyes or deny it. One way leads to happiness, another to misery. I know which road I choose," Aislinn said, meeting his eyes. Baird winced, almost imperceptibly.

"Is this where you walk away from me again?"

"I'm not so certain that I'm the one doing the walking away," Aislinn said and turned to storm across the fields.

"Sure looks like you are!" a frustrated Baird yelled after her.

Aislinn refused to respond and did her best to blink back the tears that threatened to spill onto her cheeks. It was better that she left now, she thought. Despite what the cove had tried to tell them, it was obvious that Baird wasn't her true love.

Far from it, Aislinn thought angrily and kicked at the ground before bending to gather her supplies. Her work concentration was ruined for the day, as was the light she had hoped to capture. Aislinn sliced a glance at Fiona's cottage.

Forget it, she thought. She just didn't want to hear it.

CHAPTER 16

*S*TEAM WAFTED AROUND Baird as he sat on the floor of his shower and let the water beat down on him. His bones felt chilled from his near-death experience and yet a part of him was on fire for Aislinn.

Baird closed his eyes and leaned his head back against the wall, letting the hot water pound him in the face. His mind scrambled to make sense of everything that had happened today. He tried to understand how a wave of that magnitude had slammed into him and dragged him under. For a moment there, Baird could have sworn that his heart had stopped beating. When he had heard Aislinn yell for him, he had turned to see where she was. He hadn't seen the wave coming, nor did it make a sound. The force of it was like running into a brick wall. If the cove truly was enchanted, well, it didn't pull any punches, Baird thought.

He'd rolled across the sand and vaguely remembered hitting the rock before the wave had subsided. And hadn't the water retreated as soon as Aislinn hit the beach? A part of him, not a part that he was proud of, wondered if she had done it. If she really was magickal...maybe she could do these things. Perhaps this whole thing was her just messing with his head, Baird thought.

Except...at the end there. When the cove had glowed from inside. Wow, that had just rocked his world. Baird shook his head and laughed. He must be going crazy. Nobody would believe him if he said that he saw the water glow from within. His colleagues would write him off as a nutter for sure. But, he'd watched Aislinn carefully and she'd seemed just as disconcerted and surprised as he was. The fact was, he was trained to watch for signs of lying or subterfuge and Aislinn's face had showed surprise...and dismay. He was betting money that she knew the real reason that the cove glowed from within.

Baird stood in the shower and turned the water off, stepping out to snag a towel from the rack. He brushed the towel over his body and examined himself in the mirror. Oh yeah, he was going to have a few bruises. Not to mention the cut on his head ached like a wasp's sting. At least it had stopped bleeding.

Baird wrapped the towel around his waist and walked into the kitchen, swiping a Guinness from the fridge along the way. He dropped onto the couch and pulled his iPad onto his lap.

He wasn't yet done with Aislinn, but he wasn't entirely sure of her either. His body wanted her...God, she was every fantasy he'd ever had come to life. Even his heart was ready to dive in headfirst. But Baird had long ago learned that you couldn't always trust the body or the heart's impulses. He'd seen it enough in his practice. He was going to tread carefully with Aislinn. His mind was the last holdout and Baird had about 1.2 billion questions for her.

For now, he knew his starting point. Pulling up Google, he began to research what would cause the cove to glow from within.

CHAPTER 17

*S*EVERAL DAYS LATER, Aislinn paced the shop and examined her list of inventory. She either needed to raise prices or create more products. It seemed like her work was flying off the shelves lately and her shop was beginning to look a little sparse. Unable to help herself, Aislinn peered out the front window, where she could just make out Baird's building. Cursing herself, she turned and walked away from the window.

Not a word. The man had kissed her senseless, told her that he couldn't stop thinking about her and then had just walked away. Aislinn had fully expected to hear from him after he had had a little time to process what had happened at the cove. When she hadn't, hurt had turned to anger. Anger had then turned to berating herself. Why was she mooning after a guy that she knew wasn't a good match for her? Frustrated with the contradiction of her heart and her mind, Aislinn paced the store.

"Hi, Aislinn," Morgan called from the back room.

"Hey, Morgan," Aislinn said, thankful for the distraction. Morgan had come to the shop twice to get the lay of the land and in doing so, was slowly opening up to Aislinn. Aislinn felt like she could fully trust her and the girl's exuberance was hard to resist.

"What's on the schedule for today?'

"Well, as you can see, stock is getting low." Aislinn swept her arm around the room.

"Yes, I noticed that. I have some ideas about rear-ranging it to make it look less sparse if you don't mind," Morgan offered shyly.

Aislinn thought about it. Did she mind? "Please, go ahead. In fact, I think that I am going to take the day off and go take pictures," Aislinn decided on the spot. Morgan's mouth dropped open.

"You're…just going to leave me here?"

"Yup. You know how to work the credit card machine and you have my cell number. I doubt anything too major will come up," Aislinn said.

"Wow, thanks, Aislinn, I really appreciate it."

"No problem. Now, as much as I want to get more painting done, I think that I will focus on restocking the photographs. They are easier to finish up and they sell well. Plus, the mini postcards that I make out of them fly off the shelves," Aislinn decided.

"I love your photographs. You have such a unique way of portraying things," Morgan said.

"Thank you, Morgan. Flattery will get you every-where," Aislinn laughed at her and was delighted to hear the girl's rich, pure laugh ring back.

"I'm off. Call me if you need anything," Aislinn said,

swinging her trusty Leica camera over her neck and grabbing her bag of film.

Aislinn stepped onto the street and automatically glanced
to the sky to check the light. Wispy clouds filtered the light of
the sun. Perfect, Aislinn thought, and began to walk around
the village. Though nature shots always sold well, Aislinn
found that the tourists loved pictures of anything quintessen-
tially Irish. She strolled through the village and bent to shoot
the image of a potter working in his studio through an open
window. On another pass through she caught two old men
laughing on the sidewalk in front of the pub. Aislinn zoomed
in on their faces and captured the wrinkles at the corners of
their eyes as they laughed. Continuing up the street she found
an old truck with a dog peering out of the window. Aislinn
took several shots of the dog…wide angle and up close.

Humming to herself, she continued around the village
down towards the harbor. Aislinn reached in her bag and
pulled out her long-distance lens. From the top of the hill,
a wide-angle picture of the harbor was typically stunning.
Aislinn held the camera to her face and looked through the
view finder. Movement caught her eye and she turned the
camera slightly to find it and zoomed in. Her mouth
dropped open and without thinking, she began to shoot.

Baird ran on the harbor boardwalk, shirt off, and
without his glasses. Sweat dripped from him and his
muscles gleamed in the sun. Aislinn swallowed against her
suddenly dry throat and angled in on the curve of his
pectoral muscles. Lust hummed through her body as she
continued to shoot his run. Baird stopped at an empty
bench and dropped to do triceps dips. Aislinn all but

tripped over herself as she focused on the curve of his bicep and the dip of his stomach muscles beneath the waistband of his shorts.

As if sensing he was being watched, Baird looked directly at her. Aislinn let out a little squeal and swung the camera wide, taking random shots of Flynn's restaurant. Trying to act cool, she took a few more shots and turned the camera and her body in a direction that didn't face Baird. What had she been thinking? Aislinn scolded herself as she walked behind the grocer and let out a sigh.

Silly, smitten girl, Aislinn reprimanded herself. And why was she even lusting after this man? It wasn't like he wanted to try and understand her or even make an effort to be with her.

Giving herself a mental lecture to toughen up, Aislinn shoved Baird from her mind and switched out her roll of film. She spent the next few hours walking the outskirts of the village, capturing everything from laughing nuns coming out of an old church to a solitary sheep standing on a rock. Satisfied that she'd have enough to print and frame to replenish her supply, Aislinn made her way back to the shop.

Breezing in the front door she stopped dead in her tracks.

Her shop.

What had happened to her shop?

"Do you like it?" Morgan asked nervously from the corner. Aislinn jolted. She had entirely missed the girl.

"I…I'm speechless."

"Is that bad? I can change it back," Morgan said nervously, biting at her nails.

"Are you kidding me? Don't touch a thing. This is amazing!" Aislinn squealed and ran over to give Morgan a hug. She ignored the hesitation and tension she felt in the girl's shoulders when she wrapped an arm around her. From what she could ascertain, Morgan wasn't used to being touched or comfortable with affection.

"How did you do all of this?" Aislinn exclaimed.

Morgan's face flushed.

"Oh, duh. Of course, your power. Nice work," Aislinn said casually and strolled around the room. Morgan had completely rearranged the shop. Instead of an eclectic mix of paintings and photographs shoved anywhere they would fit, there was a flow and…it made sense.

"This makes sense," Aislinn said, voicing her thoughts.

"Yes, that's what I thought," Morgan said eagerly. "I decided to group your work by your different mediums, and then by sizes and prices."

"That way if someone knows they only like watercolors…" Aislinn said.

"They'll go right to the watercolor section." Morgan finished.

"This works. The flow is better too," Aislinn said. The racks had been repositioned so that people wouldn't get bunched up by the door but instead could peruse each section easily without feeling too crowded.

"That's what I thought. I didn't want people to feel too squished and uncomfortable."

"I'm really happy with this, you've done a great job," Aislinn said.

"Did you get some good pictures today?" Morgan asked and Aislinn felt her cheeks heat.

"Um, yes, I did," Aislinn said, thinking of the pictures of Baird.

"Oh! You got a phone call from a gallery in Dublin. Something about setting up a show? I wrote it down."

Aislinn let out a screech and grabbed Morgan in another quick hug before doing a quick jig across the room and back.

"Good news, I'm guessing?" Morgan laughed at her.

"The best. My first real show! At a Dublin gallery, no less!"

"Congratulations."

"Morgan, how many days are you on Flynn's boat?"

"Whenever he needs me. It's flexible."

"Can you work more hours here over the next few weeks? I need to focus."

Morgan's mouth dropped open.

"I'd love to. Do you really trust me to do that?"

Aislinn swept her arm across the shop. "After all this? Of course I do."

A look of pure delight swept across the girl's face, and her aura shifted colors ever so slightly. Aislinn was certain that with a little love and patience, she'd be able to push the rest of the anger and loneliness from Morgan's life.

"I'll talk to Flynn tomorrow," Morgan said excitedly.

"I have to call him back." Aislinn rushed to her office.

"I'm going to leave for the day, then," Morgan called to her.

"Thanks, Morgan. See you tomorrow?"

"Yes, after I talk to Flynn," Morgan called.

Aislinn's heart was pounding so hard in her chest that she could barely hear Morgan's reply. She sat down at her desk and stared at the hastily scrawled message. She hadn't known that she had wanted to have a gallery acknowledge her work as an artist until it had happened. Aislinn had always taken great pride in selling her work on her own terms and had never craved the accolades that many of her art colleagues did. In fact, Aislinn had all but shunned that world. After art school she had simply followed her heart and been the driver of her own success. She'd seen several of her old classmates suffer rounds of rejections from galleries and she had promised herself that she would never fall into that group.

But, now this opportunity had come to her. Aislinn took a few deep breaths to steady her breathing before dialing the number on the pad.

"Green on Red Gallery, how may I help you?"

"May I speak with Martin, please?"

"One moment please," the smooth voice on the other end replied.

Aislinn doodled nervously while she waited for Martin to come to the phone.

"Yes, this is Martin." A low voice reached to her through the phone.

"Ah, yes, this is Aislinn from Wild Soul Gallery in Grace's Cove?"

"Yes, Aislinn! Thank you so much for returning my call."

"Of course, the pleasure is all mine," Aislinn gushed.

"Well, I've had the delight of meeting your mother and she has sent me pictures of your work. I'm in love! We must have you for a show. What works for you?"

Martin took for granted that she would want to show at

their gallery and Aislinn wasn't surprised. Green on Red Gallery was well known across Ireland.

"Um, I would need a little time to prepare," Aislinn stammered.

"Of course, of course. How does four weeks from now sound? I know it is a little short for planning a show, but we have a hole in our calendar, and frankly, from what I've seen in the photographs, you already have enough to show. We'd love to focus on your oil or watercolor paintings of the coast. We haven't done any moody Irish seascapes yet as usually they are so boring and typical. Yours just jump right off the page for me and I'm certain they'll sell like hotcakes," Martin said excitedly.

"Four weeks? Okay, I can do that," Aislinn said determinedly. "How many pieces would you like?"

"Hmmm, I'll try not to be greedy but say…between twenty-five and forty? Depending on their size?"

Aislinn gulped.

"Yes, sir. I can do that."

"Excellent. Give me your email address and I'll send you further details."

Aislinn rattled off her information as her hand trembled around the phone. Forty pieces to be shown at a famous gallery in Dublin! Her mind whirled at the possibilities and she stammered out her thanks before hanging up with Martin.

Aislinn bent and put her head between her legs, drawing in deep breaths. A part of her was surprised by how much this meant to her. Perhaps there was a level of validation in getting her own show that she had never realized that she had wanted or needed. But, as Aislinn examined deep inside of herself more closely, she realized that it was absolutely true. Part of her had always dreamed of this happening.

"No time to sit around and panic," Aislinn said sternly to herself and got out a pad of paper to begin making notes. She'd need to call her mother to thank her as well.

"Oh, screw it," Aislinn said and threw down her pencil. She let out a happy screech and raced around the room, hands in the air like she'd just won a race. After several loops, she stopped, breathing heavily, and laughed at herself.

"Okay, now I can be an adult about this," she told herself and went back to her list.

CHAPTER 18

BAIRD WATCHED AISLINN traipse up the hill in the village, away from him. He could have sworn that she was taking pictures of him but when he had looked, she'd been focused on Flynn's restaurant.

Part of him wanted to run after her. He wanted to ask her about her work, listen to her laugh…just to be with her.

Stretching his calves against the wall of the boardwalk, Baird thought about what his research had uncovered this week.

Which was next to nothing.

There was simply no documentation that he could find about the cove glowing. Granted, he'd stumbled on hundreds of articles about luminescent fish but they didn't just switch on and off like that. Frustrated, Baird ran his hand through his hair as he climbed the steps to his small apartment.

Refusing to believe that the cove was enchanted, Baird settled on the next explanation. Someone had rigged a light on the bottom of the cove. Baird hoped with every last ounce of himself that it wasn't Aislinn who had done so. He kept running her face through his mind...she'd been disconcerted, panicked even. Nothing about her mannerisms had suggested that she was lying.

Baird wondered who else could be behind it. The legendary Fiona would be the next choice and Baird was determined to dig a little deeper there.

In the meantime, he had his first client to get ready for.

CHAPTER 19

*a*ISLINN SPENT THE next week in the hills around Grace's Cove, focused on her painting. And, most decidedly not thinking about Baird, Aislinn thought with a huff as she jammed her paintbrush into the pot of water sitting next to her. Taking a deep breath, she calmed herself down. No need to take her angst out on her supplies.

Aislinn was in her courtyard, rinsing out her paint brushes from a day of painting the cliffs on the other side of the peninsula. She'd been moody all week and her work reflected that. Morgan said she'd never seen more stunning seascapes, and Aislinn secretly agreed with her. Maybe there was something to the old adage about artists and broken hearts.

Broken heart? Aislinn scoffed at herself. She'd been the one to walk away, she reminded herself. Baird and her simply weren't a good fit. Except, she'd trusted him with her secret. And when he'd rejected her it had hurt more than she'd expected.

A ball of shame and anger rolled in Aislinn's stomach and she clamped down on it fiercely. There was no way she was going to let Baird make her feel like less of a person. Who cared what that man thought anyway?

Aislinn crossed her courtyard to the small garden shed that she had converted into a darkroom. She had developed pictures earlier today and left them to dry. Opening the door quickly, she ducked through the dark curtains that she had nailed up to cover the entrance and conceal any last traces of light. Aislinn reached for the lamp switch on the table next to the entrance and flicked it on. A warm red glow illuminated the shed and bounced off the pictures that she had strung up.

Aislinn stood in front of them and crossed her arms, studying each critically. The one of the dog in the old truck would sell in moments and she made a note to print more. The men laughing outside the pub would also sell well and it brought a smile to her face to see their happiness. Aislinn's heart jumped a bit as she stopped in front of the pictures she had promised herself that she wouldn't develop.

In the first one, Baird was running, his face creased in concentration, sweat dripping down his bare chest. Aislinn itched to reach out and run her finger over the definition in his chest muscles. Moving to the next picture, she sighed as she looked at a close-up of Baird's flexed bicep and his chest muscles rippling as he performed a triceps dip. Stepping back, she looked at the grouping of photos objectively. From an art standpoint, they were outstanding. The way she had zoomed in and positioned each shot showed expertise…as though she was in love with her work and her subject.

Aislinn stopped.

In love?

In lust, she corrected herself and reached to tear the pictures down. Her hand lingered over the photographs. The artist in her couldn't deny what she saw printed on these pages.

"Not happening," Aislinn said out loud and pulled the prints down. Moving through the room, she pulled the rest of the prints down and placed them delicately in a file with tissue paper between each photo. She'd spend tonight framing the larger ones and have Morgan arrange them tomorrow.

Stepping out of the shed, Aislinn blinked at the last of the daylight.

"We come bearing gifts!" Keelin shouted over the fence and brandished a bottle of wine. Aislinn all but jumped out of her skin.

"Sure, and you're trying to give me a heart attack then?" Aislinn called with a laugh and waved her in. Cait followed closely behind.

Aislinn smiled at her pretty, mismatched extended family. Keelin had a newlywed glow about her that came with finding love and discovering her own unique powers over the past year. She was Aislinn's half-sister and was becoming a powerful healer in her own right. Cait, owner of Gallagher's Pub and with a talent for reading minds, and a decided contrast to Keelin's lush curves and statuesque height, laughed beside her, looking for all the world like a pixie fae.

Aislinn stopped and stared at Cait, her eyes narrowing in on the aura that surrounded Cait. There was something different about her. When she realized what it was, Aislinn gasped and tried to think about anything else.

Cait dropped the basket she carried.

"No!"

"Shit, I'm sorry, Cait, I tried not to think about it. You're not supposed to read my thoughts anyway," Aislinn exclaimed.

"No, no, no." Cait shook her head in disbelief.

Aislinn stared at Cait helplessly. Keelin danced around them in confusion and curiosity.

"What, you guys are killing me. No fair, using your powers. Spill," Keelin demanded.

"I'm pregnant," Cait whispered.

CHAPTER 20

"**W**HAT?" KEELIN SCREECHED and grabbed Cait by the shoulders. "Is this true?"

"I...I don't know. I was supposed to get my period this week," Cait said in a dazed manner. "I had planned to take a test tomorrow before we go to take my mum to her new place."

Keelin turned and narrowed her brandy-colored eyes at Aislinn. "What do you see?"

Aislinn shrugged her shoulders nervously. "I just saw something different about her aura is all," Aislinn said quickly.

"Okay, let's sit and talk about this. Mandatory girl's night," Keelin said quickly and directed them into the shop. Aislinn followed meekly, her hands still full of her pictures. She squeezed past the girls into her kitchenette and laid the file of photos on her workbench. Keelin and Cait whispered in hushed tones as they opened the wine and laid out snacks on small plates.

Keelin brushed past Aislinn and into the shop.

"Wow, this place looks amazing. I'm sorry that I haven't been down in a while," Keelin said as she walked around the room examining Aislinn's work.

"Thanks, Morgan rearranged it for me."

At that, Cait popped her head out of the back room.

"Sure, and my ears aren't deceiving me," Cait said in disbelief. "You hired Morgan?"

"Aye, I did at that." Aislinn nodded her agreement.

Curious, Cait stepped into the room and looked at what she had done.

"She knows her stuff," Cait said begrudgingly.

"I must have this," Keelin declared, standing in front of a picture of Flynn's boat docked on the other side of the cove. The water was almost glass-like and the boat was a thing of beauty.

"Aye, and we all know why you like that boat so much," Cait leered at Keelin and Keelin laughed at her. It had been the site of her and Flynn's first official date…and more. Aislinn was quite sure that Keelin had fond memories of that boat.

"No problem. Take it down and I'll wrap it up for you," Aislinn said. Aislinn turned at a long whistle from Cait.

"Whoa, Dr. Yum in full effect. If I wasn't head over heels for Shane, I'd make a play for him too," Cait declared as she looked down at the pictures of Baird.

"Let me see," Keelin demanded and muscled her way past a frozen Aislinn to grab a picture of Baird. She repeated Cait's whistle and turned to raise an eyebrow at Aislinn. "Details," she demanded.

"Um, I think we are missing the bigger picture here. Cait's pregnant!" Aislinn said.

Cait batted that away quickly. "We won't know for sure until tomorrow, so no changing the subject."

The two women crossed their arms across their chests and stared at Aislinn.

"Alright, I need a glass of wine," Aislinn concurred.

"Let's go outside, it's a nice night," Keelin said and Aislinn nodded her head. They all grabbed something to take outside and soon Aislinn's picnic bench was covered with snacks, wine, and several fat candles. Aislinn got up and walked around her small courtyard, lighting various torches and candles that she had stashed haphazardly along the fence and in between plants and sculptures.

"We have enough light. Stop procrastinating," Cait called and Aislinn laughed at her.

"Aren't you freaking out right now?" Aislinn wondered as she slid onto the bench across from the two. Keelin handed her a glass of wine and Aislinn took it gratefully.

"I'll freak out when I'm good and ready to freak out," Cait said, lifting her chin stubbornly. "Now, tell me about Dr. Yum. What happened after the night at the pub? You told me that something more happened but refused to get into details. I've been dying for a moment to come get the gossip."

"I'm surprised it took you this long," Aislinn said with a snort.

Cait flashed a wicked grin at her. "Aye, well, I've been busy with my own slice of yummy male."

Keelin's laugh tinkled across the both of them. "I've missed a lot. Tell me what happened at the pub. Who is this Dr. Yum anyway?"

Cait hurriedly filled Keelin in on what she knew while Aislinn gulped at her wine.

"And then he ran through the pub after her..." Cait finished dramatically.

"Oh stop. He did not run," Aislinn protested on a laugh.

"Oh, but he did. I was dying to get outside but I had my own drama to deal with," Cait said knowingly. She reached for the wine and then hesitated.

"Aye, and you'd better not, Cait," Aislinn said.

Keelin threw up her hands. "I don't know where to start! With Cait or you," Keelin said, looking between the two.

Cait and Aislinn pointed at each other across the table and they broke out laughing.

"Fine," Aislinn grumbled and filled them in on every last deliciously naughty detail. By the time she was done, Keelin had gulped down the rest of her wine and Cait was fanning her face.

"He is Dr. Yum," Cait breathed.

"Well, not so yum if he doesn't want to believe that Aislinn is telling the truth," Keelin said, coming to Aislinn's defense.

"Of course not. I'll get to that, but for a moment, can we all just appreciate the hotness of the sexy time with Dr. Yum?" Cait implored and Keelin laughed at her.

"Duly noted. Hot indeed," Keelin murmured and turned to Aislinn.

"Hot, yes, disturbingly so. He...he bothers me," Aislinn admitted on a sigh. She sipped at her wine and allowed the flavor to sit on her tongue for a moment.

Instantly concerned, Keelin reached out and ran her hand down Aislinn's arm.

"What do you want from all of this?"

"I…I don't know. See, that's the problem. I'm convinced he is wrong for me and yet I'm mooning around like a lovesick puppy," Aislinn said in distress.

Cait watched her knowingly.

"Seems to me like you have an itch and Dr. Yum is just the one to scratch it."

They all dissolved into giggles.

Keelin cast a worried gaze over her. Tucking her strawberry-blonde hair behind her ear, she pursed her lips nervously.

"Just say it, Keelin," Aislinn sighed.

"I…I don't know. I think you are probably doing the right thing. Giving it a little space. I'd wait and see if he comes to you."

"That's my plan. I'm certainly not running after him," Aislinn agreed and then turned her steely gaze on Cait.

Cait looked between both of them.

"I think you should show up wearing just a trench coat and nothing under it."

Keelin laughed and swatted Cait on the shoulder.

Aislinn eyed her and said, "Those are just the hormones talking."

"Eeep!" Cait squealed and leaned back to wrap her arms around her stomach.

"Aislinn, how can you tell?" Keelin asked.

"Just…I don't know. I see a new color mixed in with her aura. It blends beautifully. I suppose it could be that she is in love now, but my first instinct was pregnancy. Is that possible?"

Cait looked studiously down at her hands.

"Cait!" Keelin said.

"Well, ahem, one night, yes, we didn't use protection." Cait shrugged her shoulder. "I honestly thought it wasn't the right time of the month for that anyway."

"But, what will happen if you are? Will Shane stay with you?" Keelin asked, a worried frown creasing her face.

"Of course he will, the man's besotted with her," Aislinn said quickly. She had it on good authority that Shane was proposing tomorrow as she'd helped to pick the ring. Knowing that Cait could pluck the thoughts from her mind, she quickly changed the subject. "Tell me about the place you are taking your mom to."

"Aye, it's a good place for her. She'll have round-the-clock care and she can watch her shows all the time. I'm at peace with it," Cait said.

"Let's get together when you get back for a bite. I'll meet you at the pub," Aislinn said quickly.

"Sounds like a plan. Keelin?"

"Aye, I'm in."

Cait turned and leveled a look at Aislinn. She popped a piece of cheese in her mouth and chewed furiously. Aislinn waited.

"Morgan. What's the deal? She looked ready to kill us a few weeks ago," Cait said. She was referencing a night at the pub when Cait had tried to read Morgan's mind and Morgan had skewered them with a look of hatred.

"She's all bark," Aislinn said.

"I saw her dancing with Patrick at the wedding," Keelin said.

"Patrick has the hots for her," Cait concurred.

"I won't reveal everything that she's told me in confidence. But, she had it bad. She's an orphan," Aislinn said, figuring that detail would be something that even Morgan couldn't hide for long.

"No!" Keelin said, her face creased in sympathy.

"Hmm, I suppose that explains the anger," Cait murmured. "She's one of us, though. I can tell. I guess that had to have been hard, growing up without any help in that arena."

"I can attest to that." Keelin raised her hand.

"What can she do?" Cait asked.

"Honestly, I think far more than any of us. I wouldn't be surprised if she is another Fiona. But this is a new one." Aislinn waited for a dramatic beat. "It's telekinesis."

"No!" Both Keelin and Cait's mouths dropped open.

"Yes." Aislinn nodded at them before reaching for more wine.

"We need to have girl's nights more often," Keelin decided. "I just can't handle all of this news at once."

"Well, at least now I know why Baird is mooning around my pub at night," Cait declared.

Aislinn's stomach dropped a bit as she stared at Cait.

"He is?"

"He is. Whether that man will admit it or not, he's hooked."

CHAPTER 21

"*T*HAT MAN IS HOOKED*.*" Cait's words echoed in Aislinn's mind the next morning as she took her tea into the courtyard and stopped short. A jar of honey with a ribbon on it sat on her table. Cocking her head at it, Aislinn crossed the courtyard to lift the small note attached.

I think about you.

There was no name and Aislinn didn't need a detective to figure out that the honey was from Baird. Smiling, she held it to her heart for a second before putting it back down on the table and looking around. The street next to her shop was empty.

Honey, Aislinn thought. An unusual gift. Which appealed to her even more.

She passed the jar back and forth between her hands. So, Baird had made a move. Was the ball now in her court? Aislinn hated the confusion that surrounded Baird in her mind. Typically she just trusted her gut and followed her instincts. Yet, when it came to the delicious doctor she was totally undecided.

Which meant she would take some time to think about this gift, Aislinn decided.

She went into her shop to get ready for the day. Thinking about Cait's surprise party later that night, Aislinn detoured upstairs to look through her closet. On the chance that Baird would be there, she wanted to look good.

Aislinn pushed between her clothes until she found the dress she was looking for. Short. A deep slate gray with burgundy trim and piping at the collar, it showcased all of her best assets. She had just the right jewelry for it, too. Pulling out a string of interlocking gunmetal links, Aislinn draped it over the hanger so it hung against the gray dress. Perfect, she thought and smiled wickedly at herself in the mirror.

Hours later, Aislinn swung breathlessly into Gallagher's Pub. She'd almost run out of time before Cait was supposed to arrive. She'd had a customer that had lingered far past closing time. Unable to shove her out the door, Aislinn had waited patiently. And, boy, had the wait paid off, as Aislinn had made a four-figure sale. As soon as the customer had left, Aislinn had run upstairs, shimmied into her tight dress and left her curls tumbling down her back. She darkened her eyes quickly with a smoky shadow and threw her necklace on. And that had been that, Aislinn thought as she raced through the empty pub and into the back courtyard where everyone had been told to hide.

"Aislinn!" Keelin waved frantically from the corner where she sat nestled up to her husband, Flynn. Flynn flashed a smile at her and moved for Aislinn to sit next to them.

"You didn't tell me about this!" Keelin scolded Aislinn.

"Aye, and rightly so. You know how Cait will pluck a thought right from your mind. You've no practice with keeping secrets from her," Aislinn whispered to Keelin.

Keelin glowered at her.

"Oh stop with the sourpuss look, no need for secrets shortly," Aislinn whispered. Helpless not to, she scanned the courtyard packed with locals, looking for Baird. Like a knife sliding into her gut, her eyes locked with his. He leaned against the fence, arms crossed over a plaid button-down shirt. With the sleeves rolled up and glasses in place, he was hot enough to warm her up in all the right places. Aislinn nodded coolly at him and turned to watch the back door.

"They're here!" Patrick whispered from the door and everyone quieted. A long table of food lined one side of the fence and fairy lights had been strung up to emit a warm glow across the courtyard. It was a charming and festive turnout and Aislinn couldn't wait for Cait to come through the door.

Everyone watched avidly and as the voices approached, Aislinn clenched her hands.

Cait came through the door and stopped dead in her tracks.

"Surprise!" they all shouted and laughed at Cait's face. Aislinn could see the ring sparkling on her finger from across the courtyard and tears pricked her eyes. Oh, she was so happy for her.

The courtyard quieted as Cait said something that Aislinn couldn't hear and then she put her hands on her stomach and turned to Shane.

"Yes!" Aislinn shouted as the rest of the crowd laughed at Shane's surprised face.

"You were right," Keelin gushed to Aislinn.

"I knew it, I just knew it," Aislinn said.

Flynn raised his eyebrow at Aislinn. "What about us? Are we?"

Keelin turned and smiled at Flynn.

"We just started trying," she whispered to Aislinn.

Aislinn leaned back and focused in on Keelin's aura. It was harder to tell because she was so intertwined with Flynn. Aislinn watched their colors mix and merge for a bit and then – just for a brief moment – she saw a flicker of a third color. Her mouth dropped open and Keelin grabbed her arm.

"Am I?"

"I…I don't know. I swear for a second there, I saw something."

"Oh. My. God," Keelin whispered and wrapped her arms around Flynn.

"You can always ask Fiona, she'll know."

Keelin narrowed her eyes at her grandmother across the room. "If she knows, she hasn't said anything."

"Aye, well, in time," Flynn said gently and Keelin smiled again.

"You're right. Let's let Cait have her day," Keelin said. Aislinn noticed that Flynn moved Keelin's glass of cider away from her for good measure.

"Here she is!" Aislinn cried as Cait came running to them. Aislinn jumped up and wrapped her arms around Cait, so happy for her. Looking past Cait's shoulder, she patted Shane's arm.

"Well done, Shane."

"Well, it looks like we've both managed a surprise," Shane said, looking a little shell-shocked.

"Congratulations," a deep voice said and Aislinn felt the tiny hairs on the back of her neck stand up.

Baird had come to stand right beside her, his shoulder lightly brushing hers. She swore that she could feel his heat and her throat went dry. Swallowing quickly, she leaned down to grab her glass of Bulmer's. She let the cool liquid slide down her throat and watched Baird as he spoke to the happy couple.

He looked so at ease, confident in himself, she thought. Baird turned and seared her with a look.

"Aislinn."

"Baird," she said.

"Oh, jeez. Would you two just go have a shag and stop all this," Cait said. Shane turned to her, his mouth hanging open.

"Cait!"

"Sorry, must be hormones," Cait mumbled and was then pulled away by someone in the crowd.

"Sorry about that," Shane said, shaking his head, and followed his pregnant fiancée across the courtyard.

Flynn eyed Baird with new interest in his eyes and

Aislinn could see the beginning of an interrogation form-
ing. With a quick glance at Keelin, she silently pleaded for
help from her half-sister.

"Honey, I'm famished. Can we eat?" Keelin said to
distract Flynn. He looked down at her with love glowing in
his eyes and nodded. They both stood and made their way
to the line at the buffet. Baird quickly sat on the bench and
pulled her arm to sit next to him. Aislinn was acutely
aware that Baird had straddled the bench and that she sat
between his legs.

"Thank you for the honey," Aislinn said softly.

"You're welcome. You look beautiful. If you wore that
dress to torture me, mission accomplished," Baird said,
looking at her as if he could see straight through her dress
to the emerald green underwear she wore beneath it.
Aislinn gulped.

"Thanks, you look nice as well," Aislinn said stiffly.

Baird watched her for a moment.

"I suppose that I should apologize for my behavior at
the cove that day," Baird said.

"Which part? The part where you accused me of
manipulating the cove with my magickal powers or the
part where you walked away from me and didn't talk to me
for weeks?" Aislinn said sweetly, a bitchy look on her
face.

Baird sighed and ran his hands through his hair,
making him look even more tousled and sexy.

"I researched that. Still can't find anything on how it
lights up. It has to be rigged somehow," Baird insisted.

Aislinn's mouth dropped open.

He still didn't believe her.

"You've got to be kidding me. You still don't believe, do you?"

Baird shook his head and lifted his hands helplessly.

"You're more of a fool than I," Aislinn whispered furiously and made a move to get up.

"Wait, please, don't go," Baird said quickly.

"Why should I stay? So I can listen to you bounce your ridiculous scientific excuses and explanations off of me? Blind is what you are," Aislinn said.

"Well, what the hell, Aislinn? This is new for me," Baird whispered back, just as furious.

"If you wanted to be with me, you'd accept what I am," Aislinn whispered back.

"I barely know you!" Baird all but shouted and Aislinn reeled back as the conversation picked up in tempo around them and curious locals looked their way.

"Well, now you've gone and done it," Aislinn said.

"I don't care about them," Baird said.

"Well, I do. I live here and have known these people my whole life. And, since you barely know me and refuse to get to know me, I'm going to take my leave," Aislinn said huffily and rose, turning her backside to him. She heard his soft curse, but kept moving through the crowd, bypassing the food until she found Cait.

"I'm out," Aislinn said and bent down to kiss Cait's cheek. Cait peered around her to look for Baird.

"Alone?"

"Aye, alone," Aislinn said.

"I'm sorry. Want me to kick his arse?"

"No, mama, I'm fine," Aislinn laughed down at her and hugged Shane quickly. Slipping through the crowd, she made her way into the night.

Home, alone, to her studio. Her sanctuary.

CHAPTER 22

*A*ISLINN SHOVED THROUGH the back door of her shop, afraid that she was dangerously close to tears.

"I will not cry over that man," she said to the empty room and threw her bag on the counter. A pounding at the front door made her almost jump out of her skin.

Aislinn peered towards the front window, where a dark shadow was outlined in the lights of the street lamps. The banging grew more insistent.

She hadn't turned on a light yet and wondered if she could pretend that she wasn't home.

"I know you're in there," Baird shouted through the door.

"Is the man insane?" Aislinn muttered and ran to the front door before the entire village came to her doorstep to watch the show.

"Are you crazy?" Aislinn hissed as she unlocked the door and opened it a few inches. Baird stood before her, his chest heaving, having clearly just run straight from the pub.

"Aye, crazy for you," Baird said and pushed the door open. Aislinn stumbled back and before she could respond – or even think – Baird scooped her up to wrap her legs around his waist. Aislinn gasped as his hands squeezed her backside and pulled her tight against him. She had barely a moment to catch her breath before his lips closed in on her.

God, she'd wanted this. She'd dreamed about this for weeks now. Though in the bright light of day she could convince herself of all the reasons why they would never work, her dreams at night told her a different story.

Aislinn wrapped her arms around his neck and ran her hands through his thick hair. Baird kicked the door closed behind him with a bang and walked backwards, deftly maneuvering between her stacks of art. His lips never left hers and Aislinn felt like she was drowning in lust for him. She moaned against his mouth and opened for him, desperate for more.

Aislinn felt the edge of the desk hit her butt and Baird released her to stand between her legs. Cupping her face in his hands, he looked down into her eyes. Aislinn was mesmerized by his gaze, highlighted in the slash of moonlight that came through the window above her desk.

"I can't get you out of my head," Baird whispered against her lips.

Aislinn nodded, watching him silently.

"Please tell me that it is the same for you…that I'm not crazy," Baird said.

Aislinn nodded again, not trusting herself to speak.

"I don't know what to do about you," Baird said.

Aislinn felt herself getting angry and tried to dial it back down.

"Oh? I didn't realize that I was a problem to be solved," Aislinn said haughtily and stuck her nose in the air.

"Knock it off, you know what I mean," Baird said in frustration.

"Do I?" Aislinn reached behind her and switched on the small lamp that sat at her desk. A cozy glow enveloped them and Aislinn wanted to invite Baird upstairs to cuddle and watch an old movie. In bed. Naked.

Baird sighed and put his forehead down onto hers and just held her for a moment. Aislinn didn't know why she suddenly felt like crying, but she had to work to keep tears from her eyes.

"Listen, this isn't like me," Baird began.

"Oh? Really? I could have pegged you for a fly-by-the-seat-of-his-pants guy from a mile away," Aislinn said sarcastically.

Baird moved his hands to her throat and mock choked her in frustration.

"See? You drive me crazy. I've never had a one-night stand before," Baird admitted.

"It's not like I make a habit of them myself," Aislinn said.

"Aye, well, I meant what I said earlier...I don't know you," Baird said.

Aislinn felt her heart clench a bit.

"But I want to know you. All of you," Baird said.

Aislinn tilted her head up at him and ran her hand

down his cheek. His skin seemed to heat under her hand and she felt a shiver run through her at his words.

"I'm right here," Aislinn said and leaned in for a kiss.

Baird leaned back, leaving Aislinn hanging. She gaped at him in confusion.

"Aye, and that's the easy part for us. The rest..." Baird swung an arm out in frustration. "The rest is...muddled."

"I'd say so," Aislinn muttered.

"Listen, I'm not trying to discredit you or anything when I talk about the woo-woo stuff," Baird said and made quotation marks with his hands when he said "woo-woo."

Aislinn raised her eyebrows at him in disbelief.

"Did you just refer to my ability as woo-woo?" she asked icily.

"Ahhh, yes, and no. Your ability. The cove...all of it is a little much for me." Baird held his hand up to stop Aislinn from jumping down his throat. "But! I appreciate that you were upfront with me and for that I'm willing to give you a chance."

Aislinn slid her leg up between Baird's until it touched his package. With an evil glint in her eye, she pressed hard against him. Baird let out a little gasp.

"Want to rephrase that so as not to sound so insulting, Dr. Delaney?"

"Uh, I, mean that I think we should give us a chance. But in the real way. I want to take you on a date. Get to know you. Meet your family. All that stuff..." Baird said and watched Aislinn carefully.

Aislinn pressed her leg a little harder against him just to see him sweat for a moment and then eased off.

"Aye, so it's a courtship you're wanting then?"

"I suppose so, yes," Baird said.

Aislinn thought about it for a moment. In some respects, Baird was right. They knew very little of each other. Maybe she'd find some common ground with him that wouldn't make her so reluctant to date him. Or… maybe they'd scratch their itch and call it a day. One way or the other, Aislinn knew she couldn't go on with Baird constantly haunting her thoughts.

"Okay, I'll let you court me. On one condition," Aislinn said, meeting Baird's eyes.

"Name it."

"You have to keep an open mind. No hurtful comments about magick or people trying to pull one over on you. I'll do my best to explain it and I'll try to be understanding of the fact that you need some time to wrap your head around this stuff," Aislinn said in a rush of breath.

"Deal. But, then I have my own condition," Baird said, his voice husky.

"What's that?" Aislinn whispered, lost in his eyes.

"No sex."

Aislinn jerked back and glared at him.

"What?"

Baird cracked a smile at her. "That's the easy part for us."

"Until when?" Aislinn demanded.

"Until we decide we are ready," Baird said.

He leaned in gently and brushed his lips over hers, sending a warm tingle down through Aislinn's core. She sighed against his mouth and reached up to tug his arms.

"Want to come upstairs?"

Baird stepped away and smiled at her.

"With every ounce of my being," he said.

Aislinn jumped off the desk and stopped as she knocked a folder of her pictures onto the floor. "Shoot."

They bent at the same time to gather the pictures.

"But, I won't. I want to take you to dinner tomorrow. A real first date," Baird said as he knelt next to her to help her slide the pictures into the folder.

Aislinn looked at him in amusement.

"Don't you feel like we've already moved past some of that?"

"This matters. We matter. I want to do it right," Baird said stubbornly and then his hand stilled on a picture.

Aislinn felt her cheeks heat and she could have sworn that sweat broke out across her back as she realized what picture he was holding. Grabbing for it, she toppled onto the floor as Baird held it just out of her way.

"Well, now, that's a nice shot," Baird said in glee as he held the picture of his biceps in his hands. Aislinn groaned and covered her face with her hands.

Baird leaned over and kissed her head. "I'll be keeping this. I'll call you in the morning," he said cheerfully.

"I swear you just ran into my view," Aislinn called after him.

"Sure, I understand." Baird laughed all the way out of the door.

Aislinn groaned and shook her head. Of course, the man would find the pictures she took. She knew that she should have burned them.

CHAPTER 23

THE RINGING OF HER phone pushed Aislinn from a deep sleep. She fumbled around on her bedside table and then swore when the phone clattered from the table onto the floor.

Slitting one eye open, she glared into her barely lit room and heaved herself over the edge of the bed, snagging her cell phone from the floor.

"Hello?" Aislinn answered, accusation ringing in her tone.

"Good morning, beautiful." Baird's warm voice slid through the phone and straight to Aislinn's core. She squirmed a bit as she leaned back onto her pillows, pulling the cover up to her chin.

"It was a good morning up until a moment ago. You know…because I was sleeping. Peacefully," Aislinn grumbled.

"Not a morning person, Ash?" Baird laughed into the phone and Aislinn rolled her eyes at the ceiling.

"I have my moments. Sundays are sacred sleep-in days."

"Do you open the shop on Sundays?"

Aislinn shrugged her shoulder and then realized he couldn't see her. "Sometimes. It depends on my mood. I don't keep regular hours." Aislinn smiled. She could all but hear Baird's grimace through the phone. The lack of regular business hours would probably drive him crazy, she thought.

"How's that working out? Running your business based on mood?" Aislinn stiffened at the censure in his voice.

"Quite well, thanks. Not only am I barely able to keep my work in stock, I've been asked to give an exclusive show at a prestigious art gallery in Dublin. But, thanks for your concern, Dad," Aislinn said scathingly.

A long sigh greeted her from the other end of the line.

"Okay. I'm sorry. I didn't mean to come across as disapproving."

"Well, you'll need to get used to me doing things differently than you, Baird. I run my business the way that I want to. It hasn't failed me yet," Aislinn said.

"Point taken. And, congratulations on the show! That's marvelous," Baird said, warmth lacing his voice.

"Thank you," Aislinn said primly.

Another sigh greeted her.

"Would you like to know why I am calling you at 6:00 in the morning, aside from lecturing you about your business acumen or lack thereof?" Baird asked stingingly and a wide smile broke out on Aislinn's face. It was nice to see that Dr. Delaney could have an edge himself.

"Go ahead," Aislinn said sweetly.

"I'd like to steal you for the day. Our first real date. Can I?"

Warmth bloomed through Aislinn and the smile stayed on her face.

"And where would you be taking me for a whole day then?"

"It's a surprise."

"What's a girl to wear on a surprise date that will take her away for an entire day?"

"Something pretty. Wear something that will drive me crazy. But that you can walk in," Baird decided.

"Hmm, sexy but serviceable?" Aislinn decided.

"Perfect, I'll be there in a half hour."

Aislinn shot up in her bed.

"A half hour? That's not enough time for a surprise date. Hello?" She pulled the phone back and looked at it in awe. A dial tone greeted her and she wanted to throw her phone across the room.

"A half hour? Has the man gone insane?" Aislinn cursed steadily as she launched herself from the bed and ran to the shower. Pulling the curtain aside, she set the water to hot and ran to get a cup of coffee started. That in place, she whirled to her closet and began to dig.

Sexy but serviceable…she thought and rolled her eyes. Only a man would ask for something like that.

Digging deep in a pile of pants on the closet floor, she pulled out her dark gray skinny jeans. Flipping through her hangers, she spied a neon pink tank top with a deep V at the neckline. It fit her well and showed her best assets. The jeans fit like a second skin and left little to the imagination. Nodding, she tossed the clothes on her bed. Running past her coffeemaker, she poured a cup and took it into the shower with her, blowing on the steaming cup as she stepped under the hot water.

And laughed at the contradiction of her trying to cool her coffee in a hot shower. She shook her head at herself and placed the coffee on the edge of the shower wall and dipped her hair under the spray. It felt heavenly and did more to wake her up than her coffee would.

Though she wanted a longer shower, Aislinn had little time. Jumping out, she wrapped her sopping curls in a towel and quickly dried her body. She stepped to her vanity and considered her scents.

What would drive Baird crazy?

Her eyes settled on her vanilla body oil...the newest product that Keelin had developed for her. Aislinn could swear that she had read somewhere that the scent of vanilla was the most arousing to men.

She took the bottle and dabbed some oil on her wrists, at her cleavage and behind her ears. It smelled heavenly and made her dream about baking chocolate chip cookies and the scent filling the house.

Glancing at the clock, she swore and quickly brushed on some eye makeup before shimmying into her sexiest bra and underwear.

No sex, Aislinn reminded herself.

But, that didn't mean that Baird wouldn't see her underwear, she thought with a smirk and began to imagine all the ways that she could torture him. Aislinn pulled on her jeans just as she heard the knock on the door below.

"Coming!" she yelled.

Pulling the pink top over her head, she stood in front of the mirror and flipped her damp curls back. Aislinn ran a quick handful of gel through the curls and then clipped them back from her face, knowing they would take a while to dry. She snagged her purse and her cell phone and then skipped down the stairs.

Baird stood at her window, looking far more awake and cheerful than anyone should at this hour, and waved to her.

Of course, he was a morning person, Aislinn thought with a grumble.

She pulled the door open and squinted at him in the soft morning light.

"The only thing that I get up this early for is my art," Aislinn said.

"It's honored I am then." Baird smiled at her and held out his hand.

Aislinn turned and locked the door, making sure the closed sign was faced prominently in the window. It was too early to call Morgan to come cover for her. Her business would be fine if it was closed for a Sunday.

And wasn't that the charm and frustration of small towns? Things ran on their own terms, including her shop. Baird would have to get used to that, Aislinn thought as she reached out and took his hand.

"It's a nice morning," Baird commented as they strolled towards the water.

"Aye, I suppose it is. Though it would be better with a cup of coffee," Aislinn mumbled. Baird chuckled and brought her hand to his lips to brush a soft kiss over her knuckles. Her skin tingled at the contact.

Baird tugged her towards his car, the sedan that she had previously rolled her eyes at. Unlocking the passenger door, he held it open to show a steaming cup of to-go coffee and a bakery bag sitting on the console.

"Nothing but the best for you," Baird said dramatically and Aislinn laughed up at him.

"Okay, so you covered the bases. You get points for coffee," Aislinn said and trailed her hand down his chest to his hard abs and toyed with his belt buckle as she passed him and slipped into the car.

"You smell good," Baird breathed as she settled into the car.

"To drive you crazy, remember?"

"Mission accomplished," Baird mumbled and closed the door, coming around to the driver's side.

Aislinn snagged the bakery bag and opened it, sniffing at its contents.

"Cinnamon muffins?"

"I asked the bakery what your favorite was," Baird said with a smile.

"Aye, and set the whole town to talking, I'm sure."

"So?" Baird said and started the car, directing it out of Grace's Cove.

"So? You don't care that people will be in your business?"

"As I'm not embarrassed to be dating you, I don't see what the issue is," Baird said smoothly.

Aislinn shoved a piece of muffin in her mouth to keep from answering.

Baird smiled at her and reached over to flip the radio on. A bluesy sort of soul music came piping out of the speakers and Aislinn found herself instantly mellowed. At the very least, he had good taste in music.

"Do you not date a lot? Here?" Baird asked casually.

Aislinn choked on her muffin and reached for her coffee to clear her throat.

"Um, it's not so much that. I've just learned to keep things under wraps in a small town until...you know." Aislinn shrugged.

"Until what?" Baird asked smoothly.

"Until, you know...things are official. That you're a couple, is all."

"And what would happen if people knew you were dating someone casually?" Baird asked, curiosity lacing his voice.

Aislinn shrugged and tore off another piece of the cinnamon muffin.

"I suppose that nothing would happen, not really. Certain people in town might suggest that I have a reputation for being fast, is all," Aislinn said.

"And that bothers you," Baird stated.

"Yes, Dr. Delaney. Am I in a session right now?" Aislinn asked. She turned to raise her eyebrow at him and caught a quick flash of his grin.

"Not in the slightest, though you do sound rather defensive, if you'd like my professional opinion."

"Seeing as how I haven't asked for it...no, I don't at that," Aislinn said and crossed her arms over her chest.

"I like your outfit," Baird said, smoothly changing the topic.

"Do you?" Aislinn pushed her arms under her breasts so her cleavage pushed up against the pink shirt and angled herself so he'd have a good look. The car jerked as he lost himself in the view for a moment. Aislinn laughed as he swore and righted the wheel.

"Trying to get us killed?" Baird asked.

Feeling like they were back on even ground, Aislinn reached in the bag and handed him a muffin.

"Here, have a muffin. You must get cranky when you don't eat," she said generously.

Baird's face looked thunderous for a moment and then he broke out in a loud chuckle, the sound bouncing around the car over the music.

"I must, at that," he concurred and snagged the muffin from her hand.

Their banter continued over the hour as the sea disappeared behind them and they cut over the hills towards central Ireland.

"And where are you taking me?" Aislinn asked.

"Killarney," Baird said.

"Killarney? Why?"

"Because I've never been and I've heard it's lovely."

Aislinn twisted to look at him. "You've never been to Killarney?"

"No, but I've been to the States several times. Does that make up for it?"

"Where?" Aislinn asked immediately, pouncing on the question.

"New York City," Baird began and Aislinn cut him off, clutching at her chest.

"Ugh, just ugh. I'm dying to go to New York City!" Aislinn gushed.

"Really? Why? I'm surprised at that…small-town girl such as yourself," Baird said.

"Small town doesn't mean small minded, might I remind you," Aislinn said. "I could lose myself in the galleries alone."

"I suppose for an artist it would be wonderful," Baird admitted.

"I've always wanted to visit the Guggenheim," Aislinn admitted.

"It is amazing. The building itself is a sculpture, the way the floors circle up. When I went they had four of the Terracotta Warriors there. It was phenomenal to see."

Aislinn's mouth dropped open.

"You like art?"

Baird shrugged his shoulders. "Sure, who doesn't? What…you thought that I couldn't understand art?"

Aislinn's mouth opened and closed a few times as she considered her words carefully. "It's not that I thought that you couldn't appreciate art. I guess that I just figured that art wasn't on your radar. That it was something more for the free-flowing, less rigid types."

"Less rigid?" Baird pounced on her words and Aislinn saw his hands tighten on the wheel.

"Well, yeah. I mean, you're kind of Type A," Aislinn said.

"I am not," Baird said stiffly.

Aislinn felt the laugh bubble up from deep in her stomach and she slapped a hand over her mouth, trying desperately to stop the sound, knowing that Baird would be deeply offended. Her nose squeaked unattractively as she held her hand over her mouth and the sound made her giggle even more.

"Oh just stop, fine, I'm a little rigid," Baird admitted and Aislinn let out a whoosh of air and giggles as she reached over and ran her hand affectionately over Baird's arm.

"A little? I'm fairly certain you've ironed those jeans you're wearing."

Baird looked down at his jeans in confusion.

"What's wrong with ironing jeans?"

Aislinn threw up her hands and laughed even harder.

"And that is why I am quite certain that we can never progress past dating. There are two types of people in the world: those who iron their jeans and those who pull them from a crumpled ball on the floor," Aislinn said, sweeping her hands down to encompass her gray skinny jeans.

"Those don't look wrinkled."

"Aye, 'cause they have stretch. But, still," Aislinn said, leaning back into the seat, feeling a little smug that she'd been right.

"I'm not always Type A. I surprised you with an impulsive trip, didn't I?" Baird asked.

"That I bet you have planned to a T," Aislinn followed up smoothly and was rewarded with Baird's mouth dropping open.

"Simply to make the best use of our time is all," Baird defended himself.

"Why don't you let me take the reins today, Doctor?" Aislinn asked, testing him.

"But...I...but," Baird sputtered and then turned to see Aislinn grinning madly at him.

"Fine," Baird spit out.

"Oh, boy, this is going to be fun," Aislinn crowed, thinking that 8:00 am on a Sunday wasn't looking so bad after all.

CHAPTER 24

"*J*ARVEYS?" BAIRD ASKED in confusion as he eyed up the line of jaunting cars that stood in a row on the street, proud horses stamping their feet, drivers laughing in a group.

"Yes, a jaunting car. Come, you'll love it," Aislinn said and pulled Baird towards a driver.

"You all full up?" Aislinn asked.

"Nope, a slow one this morning. Services." The driver motioned to the church next door where Sunday services were running.

Aislinn immediately felt the guilt that always came with skipping mass and she said a quick prayer in her head before smiling up at the driver.

"A quick one, then? Ross Castle?"

"Sure, and that's an easy drive on a nice day," the driver agreed and motioned to his car. He stood at the side and held out his hand to hoist Aislinn into the cart, and Baird hopped up easily after her. They sat on the long wood bench, nestled against each other, as the driver patted his horse down before hopping into his seat, his back to them.

"And I'm sure you know the history of Ross Castle, then," the driver began.

"No, we don't." Aislinn cut Baird off and grinned up at him as the driver launched into a detailed and highly animated story about Ross Castle. Aislinn found herself hooting in laughter at some of his more exaggerated tales.

The car wound down a lane and towards an old castle tucked on the shores of a still lake that stretched wide, mirroring the trees and the sky. Sweeping trees stood at the back of the castle and Aislinn smiled at the beauty of it. Holding her hands up, she framed the shot for a mental image to paint from later.

Baird tilted his head at her in question.

"Just memorizing the picture. I can paint from memory." Aislinn shrugged, feeling foolish.

"As in you can paint the exact details or a concept of it?" Baird asked, his slate eyes glinting at her in the soft light of the morning sun.

"Like I can paint exactly…I kind of have a photographic memory of sorts for images," Aislinn said.

"That's impressive. Why do you paint out in the hills then?" Baird asked. Aislinn leaned her head on his shoulder and thought about it as the cart rolled to a stop.

"I think because I prefer the mood of being there in person. Though I can remember all the details, I read the colors and energy when I am in a particular spot. It adds a dimension to my painting that isn't always there if I just paint from memory."

Aislinn didn't have to look at Baird's face to feel his

disbelief radiating from him. She sat up and turned away from him, smiling brightly to the carriage driver as he held up his hand to help her down.

"I'll give you a half hour or so to poke around?" the driver asked.

"That's perfect." Aislinn beamed at him and picked up her pace a little, forcing Baird to catch up with her as they approached the weathered stone castle.

"Aislinn," Baird said quietly.

"Yes?" Aislinn turned, a wide smile plastered on her face.

"You're angry with me," Baird said.

"Nope, not at all," Aislinn said and took his hand, deliberately ignoring her feelings as she pulled Baird through an arched doorway to a stone staircase that hid a small door in the pocket beneath it. The energy and history of the building pulsed at her and Aislinn found it hard to stay mad at Baird when she wanted to get swept away in the memories of the castle.

"You are," Baird insisted, pulling her back against his chest for a moment. Aislinn closed her eyes, knowing that she would have to have the conversation with him soon.

Why not now?

Turning, she met Baird's eyes.

"Baird, the natural world has energy that I can feel. Just like I could feel your disbelief in the cart. Just like I can feel the history of this place. I can see it, feel it, paint it…it's all part of who I am. My gift."

Aislinn watched as Baird's eyebrows rose and a polite smile fell across his lips. This must be his psychiatrist face, she thought. Polite interest when inside he thought she was nuts.

"Stop!" Aislinn shouted and Baird's hands came up automatically to shush her.

"Shh, stop what?" Baird asked, his mouth dropping open in surprise.

"Stop…that look. Your polite doctor look. I know what you feel. I can feel it. Do you get that? I know that you are trying to be patient with me but you completely don't believe in anything that I am saying. It's insulting. You could at least pretend to humor me."

Baird's hands dropped to his sides. "I…I thought that was what I was doing."

"You're not doing a very good job of it," Aislinn said and walked away from him, tracing her toe in the dirt as she thought about how she wanted to handle this situation.

Handle him.

Turning, she crossed her arms over her chest and looked at him across the courtyard. Frustration radiated from him. She could see it in the way he stood, all sexy and rumpled and angry. Thrown him off his course is what she'd done, Aislinn thought.

But underneath it…she could see it.

He cared about her.

It wasn't love. Maybe not yet. Maybe not ever. But it was the beginnings. She could see it peeking out beneath all the confusion of his surface emotions. That was enough to make her stop and consider.

"Here's the deal," Aislinn said, walking slowly back towards him. "Today, I'm going to vocalize everything that

I see and feel. I'm used to tuning it out so that I barely pay attention to it that much unless I am immersed in my art. But, today, I'm going to show you all of me. You just need to stop trying to figure me out for the day and listen, okay?"

Aislinn stopped in front of Baird and tilted her face up to look at him. He seemed to mull over her words for a moment, which she appreciated. He cared enough to take her seriously and to think about his answer.

"I can do that. I'm sorry, I'm not trying to hurt you. I just have a hard time with all of this," Baird said and ran his hands down her arms. Aislinn tried not to bristle at his words.

"All of this? *This*…is me. It isn't a thing that is separate from me that you can analyze. It's just me," Aislinn said, needing him to understand that concept. "It's offensive to me when you refer to my gift…my essence…as "woo-woo" stuff."

Baird stiffened and Aislinn could feel the shame wash through him.

"I'm sorry. I am. I wasn't thinking of it like that. I've gone and been right judgmental, haven't I?"

"A wee bit," Aislinn said, smiling up at him.

"I'm sorry for that. I'll keep an open mind. Wow me with your gift, oh great one," Baird teased.

Aislinn laughed and threw her arms around his neck, reaching up to brush a kiss over his lips. She squealed into his mouth as he wrapped his arms around her waist and lifted her in a dizzying spin, deepening their kiss.

"Sure and it's nice to see some lovebirds," their driver

called to them and they broke apart, laughing at getting caught.

Love, Aislinn thought. She wondered if she was on the tipping point and then shook the thought from her mind. It wouldn't do to fall for Baird. She'd only get hurt.

CHAPTER 25

*H*OURS LATER, AISLINN stretched out her legs in the grass of a park and leaned against a tree, enjoying the sunshine that fell across her face. A giggle snorted out unattractively through her nose, and she slapped a hand over her mouth and slanted a look at Baird.

He raised an eyebrow at her, his face set in a scowl.

She hadn't meant to tip the canoe.

The black swans had shocked and excited her. In her rush to get a better look at them…she may have leaned too far from the boat.

Another snort slipped from her and she heard Baird grumble next to her.

"Pizza?"

Aislinn smiled sweetly at Baird and handed him a slice from the takeout box she had grabbed from the pizza joint across from the park.

Baird took the slice silently and Aislinn handed him a napkin with it.

"Probably a far cry from what you had planned for

lunch, huh?" Aislinn said easily as she bit into her slice. The heavenly taste of pepperoni and cheese filled her mouth and she groaned around the pizza, losing herself in the taste.

She really needed to eat pizza more often, Aislinn decided.

Baird sniffed and took another bite. "I'd only planned lunch at one of the best restaurants here. Wine, steak, linen tablecloths..."

Aislinn shrugged and bumped his shoulder with hers.

"This is nice." She gestured to the park with her slice of pizza.

"I suppose it is," Baird admitted. "Good pizza."

"It is at that. I try to get to this place once in a while. It's worth a trip."

"I can't believe you flipped the canoe," Baird said indignantly.

Aislinn snorted again and then let the laughs roll from her gut. Bending over, she slapped her sodden jeans and then looked over at Baird. His clothes were a mess, wrinkled, stained, and his hair was all mussed up.

He'd thought to grab his glasses as they tipped. He had good instincts, Aislinn thought. She liked seeing him like this. Mussed, out of his element.

Like a real person.

"I really didn't mean to tip it. You'd think that I'd know better, having been raised on the water. I can get a little exciteable at times," Aislinn admitted.

"I see that," Baird said stiffly and Aislinn laughed at him.

"I like you like this," Aislinn admitted.

"Oh yeah? Then I think you owe me," Baird said. He reached out and snatched Aislinn under the arms and pulled her until she sprawled across his body. Her slice of pizza went flying and Aislinn glared at him.

"Hey! My pizza."

"I'll buy you another slice," Baird said and pulled her tight against him, crushing her lips in a searing kiss. Instant heat shot through her and Aislinn forgot about the pizza, about their wet clothes, and lost herself in the kiss. Baird kissed like he did everything else, with complete concentration on the task at hand, and with a dedication to ensuring their pleasure.

She gasped against his mouth, craving more, wanting all of him.

Baird eased back and held her there, his eyes boring into hers.

"See? I can be impulsive." Baird's lips twitched in a smile and Aislinn's heart cracked open…just a bit more.

"I'm impressed, Dr. Delaney. I wouldn't have expected you to be so brazen in public. In front of children, no less." Aislinn hooted out a laugh as Baird's cheeks pinked and he looked hurriedly around for kids.

"Teasing…" Aislinn said breathlessly, happy to break the intensity of the moment.

Baird reached up and ran a hand down her nose, tracing her lips and then her cheeks.

"Your face. It's so beautiful. Such a contradiction. Much like yourself. Yet it all fits together to make something so unusual and interesting."

Struck by his words, Aislinn eased back from him.

Afraid to spill too much, afraid that she would do something impulsive like ask him to be with her. Forever.

"Thank you, I find you handsome as well," Aislinn said and moved to sit next to him.

"Yes, I can see that, since you stalk me and take pictures of me," Baird said and Aislinn groaned and threw her hands up.

"I most certainly did not. I was photographing the village and life in the village. You are alive. In the village. That is all," Aislinn said determinedly and took another piece of pizza from the box.

"Uh huh, you want my body, don't you?" Baird teased her.

Aislinn groaned and turned and stuck the piece of pizza in Baird's laughing mouth. They both convulsed in laughter at their actions. Leaning companionably back against the tree, Aislinn interlaced her fingers with his.

"Thanks for bringing me today, I needed some time away," Aislinn said.

"You're welcome. Tell me what you see," Baird demanded, spreading his arm out to the park.

She'd been giving him a run-down all day long of what she sensed and felt and the more in depth she had gotten, the more Baird had seemed to listen and care about what she said.

Aislinn focused on two businessmen walking by in suits.

"See those two? They are both anxious about something. Maybe a business or realtor deal. You can tell by the way they walk, but it is more in the vibe that I get from them. Something is wrong in their world."

Aislinn turned and watched a young family stroll by.

"The parents? They've just had a fight. Their energy shows that there is a lot of anger and frustration at the surface, but underneath, a really strong love. The love is already overtaking the frustration and I bet by the time the walk is over it will be gone. The dad is really proud of his little boy and the mom has a special love for her baby in her arms. The baby is still really connected to her so their colors mingle in a maternal bond kind of way."

Aislinn shoved away the thought of having a child. She hadn't realized that she had maternal urges, especially coming from the messed up family that she had come from. But, every once in a while, it was there. Just a hint of it, poking through, tweaking her heartstrings.

"And what about them?" Baird gestured to an old man and a woman that sat on a bench, holding hands.

"Well, aren't they just a sweet picture?" Aislinn said.

"Aye, they are."

Aislinn turned to look at him.

"What do you see?" Aislinn asked him.

"I see love. A love that doesn't care about looks, that has survived battles, that has seen hardships and troubles, that has been tested and grown stronger for the testing, and one that will last on…into the grave." Baird spoke softly and Aislinn felt tears prick her eyes at his words.

"Aye, you don't need me to tell you those things," Aislinn whispered.

"Tell me anyway," Baird said.

"They are the same. It isn't often you see a bond like theirs. Their colors and energy have blended and become interwoven until they are like a braid or a chain. This strong, pure love runs between them, and it has connected them forever. They're soul mates," Aislinn said simply.

"What happens when one goes?" Baird asked.

"The other follows quickly. They are for each other," Aislinn said and shrugged her shoulders.

"Do you believe in that? In afterlife? Ghosts and such?"

Aislinn tilted her head up to look at the fat cottonball clouds that chugged through the crystalline blue sky. It was a perfect day, a little slice of heaven on earth.

"I do. But, probably in a different way than most. Because I can feel the energy of the earth...of this day." Aislinn swept her arm around to the park. "And I've been exposed to some of the mystical workings of those that have gone before us. Yes, I do. I believe in an afterlife, just as much as I believe that there are spirits and ghosts."

"Hmmm," Baird commented.

"You don't believe in ghosts?" Aislinn leaned forward and looked at Baird in disbelief. "Why, that's positively un-Irish."

Baird laughed at her and she sat back against the tree, the bark scratching lightly into her back.

"There's an energy to everything. I don't know if you want to call it a universal force or call it God, but it's there. In the way the trees pulse with movement to the way that love flows around that couple. It's there."

"I suppose that there is something to all of it, of course," Baird said.

"Baird...how can we ever really date if you don't believe in what I am?" Aislinn asked, a little hitch in her voice.

"It's not that I don't believe in what you can do. I just don't understand it. Why can one person have this ability but another doesn't? I'm of a skeptical mind, Aislinn, so when science can't prove something...then what am I supposed to think?"

"Do you believe in God?"

"Of course," Baird answered automatically.

"But science can't prove that he exists," Aislinn said.

"That's where faith comes in," Baird said, his years of being an Irish Catholic showing through.

"Exactly," Aislinn said quietly.

CHAPTER 26

*B*AIRD THOUGHT ABOUT her words on the drive home. The sun was setting on the edge of the countryside and pink rays shot up into the clouds, looking as heavenly and majestic as a picture could get.

Why could he have faith in God but not faith in the fact that Aislinn was touched with an extra gift?

He shot a glance at her. She leaned against the window, her eyelashes fanning out across gorgeous cheekbones, her chest rising in an even rhythm. Her riot of curls was pulled back in a knot and he wanted to take her hair down and run his fingers through it.

To scoop her into his arms and keep her there forever.

She did something to him. Tested him. Forced him to think outside what he had been taught. Aislinn was a fascinating and multi-talented woman. He wondered how it would work if they were together. Forever.

He thought of her description of the old woman in the park. It hadn't been much different than his, yet hers had been based on what she had felt and his on what he could see.

Was that so bad? Maybe there wasn't anything wrong with someone moving through life reacting to emotions instead of what could be seen on the surface.

It still itched at Baird, though. The why.

He wanted to know more.

Baird thought about his colleagues that he had spoken with in Dublin. Maybe he would drop them another line and dig a little further. He was certain they'd be able to shine a little light on Aislinn's ability.

Or maybe he was barking up the wrong tree.

Did he need to start with Grace O'Malley? The cove was named after her. From whence the light came, he muttered to himself.

The light.

What did it mean?

CHAPTER 27

"*A*RE WE HOME?" Aislinn asked in surprise as she felt the car come to a stop.

"Aye, we are," Baird confirmed, a smile playing lightly across his lips.

"Gosh, I'm sorry that I fell asleep. I hope that I didn't snore," Aislinn said.

"Great, big snores," Baird confirmed.

"Stop it!" Aislinn squealed and punched him lightly on the shoulder. Baird captured her hand with his, pulling it close to his face to dance a kiss across her knuckles. Aislinn's insides quivered and she lost herself for a moment in his eyes.

"Come home with me," Aislinn breathed.

"I'll walk you home," Baird clarified with a smile.

Aislinn rolled her eyes and pulled her hand away, getting out of the car in a huff. She slammed the door a little harder than necessary and crossed her arms over her chest. She didn't turn when she heard Baird's door close.

"I can walk home by myself just fine," Aislinn said, unaccountably angry.

"Nonetheless, I shall walk you home," Baird said and stepped next to her as she moved up the street.

"I'm an adult, you know," Aislinn said stiffly.

"I'm aware. But I asked you on a date and as such, I will deliver you home."

Aislinn rolled her eyes and pushed her hair back from her face.

"I meant that I'm an adult. I can sleep with whomever I want. Whenever I want," Aislinn said.

Baird turned and met her eyes. "Aye, I'm aware."

"You've heard the adage about a woman scorned..." Aislinn trailed off huffily.

Baird let out a peal of laughter that had people across the street looking their way.

"Sure, and you don't think that I'm rejecting you, do you?"

"Seems that way," Aislinn said stiffly as they neared her shop.

"I've a mind to show you just how much I want you, Ash," Baird growled as they got to her shop.

Heat flashed through her and Aislinn pulled him around the corner of her shop, towards her courtyard. Maybe tonight wouldn't be a loss after all.

"Don't touch me!" Morgan's voice shattered her cloud of lust, and ice shot through Aislinn's veins. She raced to the fence, but Baird was quicker.

"Hands off, Patrick!" Baird thundered over the fence.

CHAPTER 28

"*W*HAT'S GOING ON here?" Aislinn shouted over the fence and raced to swing the creaky wooden door open.

"Nothing! I was going to kiss her, that's all!" Patrick held his hands up. He stood away from Morgan, his face pink with embarrassment.

Aislinn flipped her gaze to Morgan. The girl looked like she was huddled in on herself, her hands wrapped tightly over her chest, her eyes on the ground. Aislinn did a quick scan of her emotions.

Shame.

She turned to Patrick and read him too.

"What were you thinking?" Baird yelled and made to move past Aislinn to Patrick. Aislinn blocked his movements with her arm, hitting what felt like a solid wall of muscle.

"Stop," Aislinn said quietly and was glad that Baird responded instantly.

"What?" He turned to look at her, waiting.

A little sliver of happiness slid through her. Whether he realized it or not, Baird was taking into account her gift.

"He's embarrassed but has no intent to harm. There's something else going on here," Aislinn whispered.

Baird lifted his eyes and scanned the two and then nodded down at her.

"Want me to take him for a walk? Cool him down?"

"Please," Aislinn said.

"Patrick, let's go for a walk. Maybe grab a pint?" Baird asked jovially and Patrick nodded, grateful for the reprieve.

Aislinn moved towards Morgan, patting Patrick softly on his back as he passed her. She didn't touch Morgan, just stood next to her for a moment.

"Some tea?"

"No, I should go," Morgan insisted, finally meeting Aislinn's eyes.

Aislinn felt a lash of pain slice through her and for a moment, she felt all of Morgan's humiliation and anger. The force of it almost brought tears to her eyes but she knew that tears wouldn't help Morgan.

"Wine, then," Aislinn insisted. Scanning the courtyard, she realized that Morgan needed something else.

"Come on, upstairs." Aislinn motioned to her apartment.

"I...I should go. You're my employer. I'm sorry this happened here," Morgan shuddered out.

"I'm more than your employer, as I've told you many a time. Now, upstairs," Aislinn ordered briskly and Morgan nodded. The girl darted across the courtyard and waited for Aislinn at the door. Fishing her keys from her purse,

Aislinn tried to keep her mind off what would have happened with Baird and her.

She led the way up her stairs, flipping the lights on as she went. Aislinn gestured towards her couch in the living room and Morgan fled there to curl up in a ball. Aislinn raised an eyebrow at her but didn't comment. Instead, she moved into her small kitchen and pulled out two glasses and a bottle of Chianti.

"Red okay?"

"Sure," Morgan said quietly and stared down at her hands.

Aislinn moved to her coffee table, a long piece of reclaimed wood that ran the length of her low-slung couch. She nudged a few sketchbooks out of the way and placed the wine in front of Morgan. Aislinn sank back into the couch and studied Morgan for a moment.

She sipped her wine and considered her approach. Morgan had already made it clear that much of her story was off limits, though she'd slowly opened up more over the weeks of working part-time for Aislinn.

"I don't know how to date guys," Morgan blurted out.

Aislinn raised her eyebrows in surprise and then decided to remain silent. She sipped her wine as she waited for more from Morgan.

"My...my last foster home...before I took off? The son of the house..." Morgan's lip trembled and Aislinn felt her entire body tense.

"Did he rape you?" Aislinn hissed.

Morgan raised shocked eyes to Aislinn.

"No, no, no...nothing like that," Morgan said and

reached for her wine. She took a hurried sip and then put it down, wrapping her arms around her legs again.

"I had a crush on him. A huge crush on him. He was older than me and popular. All the girls thought he was so great. I even became a little more popular at school because we lived in the same house."

Aislinn nodded, encouraging Morgan to speak more.

"I'd...I'd never been kissed before him," Morgan explained.

"That's okay, I didn't have a lot of romances as a teenager either," Aislinn said.

"Well, one day, behind school, he pulled me aside and leaned in to kiss me. I closed my eyes and leaned in...and just when I thought he would kiss me...he bent and pulled my skirt down. He hooked my underwear along the way and...I was naked from the waist down."

Morgan gulped at the memory and Aislinn wanted to beat up the little prick that had done this to her.

"I should have seen it coming, but I was so absorbed in the thought of him kissing me that I missed his thoughts on what he planned to do. It wouldn't have been so bad. I could have handled it, except he'd called all the popular kids out to watch. I just remember turning and seeing the girls screaming and pointing and laughing and the guys high-fiving him. I ran all the way home." Morgan shrugged her shoulders and took another sip of wine. "School was hell after that. Everyone was mean to me. It was like he'd given them permission to bully me. I took off a few months after that and have been on my own ever since."

Aislinn wanted to hug her and tell her it was going to

be okay. That everyone had awkward teenage years and that more than one of them had scars that would last.

A smile flitted across Morgan's beautiful face and Aislinn raised her eyebrow in question.

"Well, I did…uh, get my revenge," Morgan snickered.

"Uh oh," Aislinn said and took a hurried sip of her wine.

"The day that I left? Well, his mum had prepared a huge spaghetti lunch for him and then left to go to the market. I'd packed my bags and had my bus ticket. Everything was outside and I'd left a short note so they knew that I'd gone off on my own. But, I stopped in the kitchen on the way out. God, I still remember his face. He just looked at me like I was dirt. I smiled at him…very sweetly…and then raised the plate with my power and dumped it on his head."

Aislinn's mouth dropped open.

Morgan let out a laugh and happiness lit across her face for a moment, making her breathtakingly beautiful.

"God, I've never seen anyone's face change so quickly. He jumped up to run and then slipped in spaghetti and fell." Morgan laughed even harder. "I know it's wrong. Trust me, I know. But…just that once, it was worth it."

Aislinn knew that she should probably school her on proper use of her power, as Fiona would advise, but Aislinn had to give Morgan this one. The little jerk had deserved it.

"Though I wouldn't advise doing that again as you don't need a modern-day witch hunt on your hands, I agree, he deserved it."

Morgan smiled at her and Aislinn could feel gratitude

radiating from her. She wiggled against the cushions, burrowing further into the pillows.

"So, Patrick?" Aislinn asked.

"Patrick," Morgan said and her body tensed.

"You like him," Aislinn stated. She could read it.

"I do. I just...freaked when he tried to kiss me. It was like déjà vu. A cute guy, behind the house, in the court-yard." Morgan sighed and sipped her wine. "I need to learn to control my emotions better."

"It's okay to be emotional. But, yes, you probably have some stuff to work through. Maybe you could talk to Dr. Delaney?"

Morgan raised her eyebrow at Aislinn and laughed.

"Like I have money for that."

"I might be able to work something out," Aislinn said.

"What's up with you and him anyway?"

Aislinn thought about it for a moment.

"Let's just say that I don't scream when he tries to kiss me."

CHAPTER 29

"*I* swear that I didn't do anything," Patrick said as he paced along beside Baird, his feet stomping the pavement.

"What happened?" Baird asked stiffly, reserving judgment.

"Nothing at all. We've been talking more. I'll see her here and there and…man, she's just a knockout. I'm drawn to her, you know? I've stopped dating and am kind of, like, trying to get her to go on a date with me."

Baird nodded and held the door open to Gallagher's Pub. Patrick waved a hello to the bartender and ducked under the pass-through to snag two Guinness bottles from the bin.

"Put it on my tab," he instructed the bartender and then moved back around, motioning for Baird to follow him back into the courtyard.

They sat at an empty picnic table. The courtyard was empty as the night was still young.

"So, how did you end up in the courtyard?"

"I saw Morgan hefting a couple of huge pieces of drift-wood up the street. For what? I don't know...but I offered to help her take them into the courtyard. I just figured it was for one of Aislinn's art projects. Then, I don't know, it was like, the right moment, you know? Sun just setting, she looked so pretty, and I wanted to kiss her. I didn't expect her to scream at me. I thought she was feeling the same way." Patrick shrugged his shoulders to dismiss it. Baird could see that his shoulders were tense and he read frustration and hurt across the young man's face.

"I'm sure that there is more to the story. From what Aislinn has said, Morgan's had a rough upbringing. Be patient with her," Baird said.

"Oh yeah, like what?"

"I'm not at liberty to say," Baird said smoothly.

Patrick smiled at him. "Doctor confidentiality?"

"Something like that," Baird agreed.

The men drank their beers in silence for a moment. Realizing that this might be the perfect moment to raise a question, Baird studied Patrick.

"Did you grow up here?"

"Aye, I did."

"Is the cove enchanted?

Patrick didn't even blink an eye. "Yes."

Baird banged his Guinness bottle down on the table in surprise. "Yes? Just yes? You believe it?"

"Aye, why wouldn't I?" Patrick looked at him in confusion.

"I don't know...maybe because it's crazy to think that there is magick there?"

"There's magick everywhere," Patrick said simply.

Baird looked around him in disbelief and worked on finding the right words.

"I just...I feel like everyone in this town is a little nuts," Baird confessed.

Patrick grinned at him, unoffended.

"Aye, well, when a town has some magick in it, what do you expect? I like it though, it makes us unique."

"What's the story...the Grace's Cove thing?"

"Story goes that she died there. Protected the cove with magick and gave her descendants a little extra something special." Patrick shrugged it away and took another sip of his Guinness.

Baird's mouth hung open. "You're telling me you believe this then?"

"Sure, ask Cait. She's a descendant. She can read minds," Patrick said easily and gestured to Cait walking through the door.

Baird immediately stood as she moved to join them.

"Congratulations again, Cait. How are you feeling?" His mind wheeled frantically as he tried to digest what Patrick had just told him. There was no way that she could read minds.

"Oh, jeez, Patrick. You told him?" Cait narrowed her eyes at Patrick and he hunched his shoulders in guilt.

"Sorry, Cait. He was asking about the cove and it just kind of went from there. I figured he already knew since he's been spending so much time with Aislinn."

Cait turned to look Baird up and down.

"Hmpf," she murmured, and motioned for Baird to sit again. "You, go. There's a shipment that needs to be unpacked." Cait jerked her thumb at Patrick and then back towards the pub.

"Yes, ma'am. Thanks for listening, Baird," Patrick said as he scurried from the courtyard.

Cait met Baird's eyes and he was struck again by the intelligence and presence he saw there. This was a woman that knew her own worth.

"Thank you," Cait said simply.

Baird's eyebrows rose as he realized that Cait had scanned his thoughts.

"I...I'm sorry. But, can you really do that?"

"I don't know, can I?" Cait said snarkily.

Baird tilted his head in annoyance at her and she sighed, rubbing her hands over her small stomach.

"Sorry, hormones make me a little bitchy. Yes, I can read minds. Yes, I'm a descendant of the great Grace O'Malley, the one and same who both cursed and enchanted the cove."

"This is all so fantastical to me. It's the stuff of fairy-tales," Baird blurted out.

Cait shrugged her shoulders. "I suppose that it is. I can't change it though. Not sure that I'd want to anymore..." She trailed off and looked down at her belly and smiled. "This kid of mine isn't going to be able to pull anything on me." A wicked grin lit across her pretty face and Baird found himself smiling in response.

"I suppose that will come in handy as a mother," Baird conceded.

"What are your intentions towards Aislinn?" Cait asked directly.

Baird blew out a breath and took a long pull from his bottle of beer. What were his intentions?

"I don't know," he said finally.

"Then leave her alone," Cait said, fury darkening her face.

Baird held his hands up to stop Cait from going further. "I don't know, but I want to find out. There is something about her that fascinates me, hooks me in, that I want to learn more of. She is pushing me outside of my comfort zone and I'd like to think that I am doing the same for her. For what it's worth, my intentions are honorable. I've turned her down, more than once," Baird said, not feeling the need to explain more.

Cait hooted in laughter at that.

"Aye, I'm right sure that must have made her mad."

"Spitting mad. She's even more beautiful when she's mad," Baird said with a smile.

"Take your time with her," Cait cautioned.

"Tell me about the cove," Baird said.

"What about it?"

"Why does it glow blue?"

Cait coughed and crossed her arms over her chest. Leaning back, she glared at Baird.

"Who were you with when that happened?"

"How do you know that I wasn't alone?" Baird countered.

Cait's face pokered up even more. She didn't say a word.

"Fine, I was with Aislinn," Baird sighed and finished his beer, getting sick of trying to figure out all of the mysteries and riddles in this town.

A quick smile flitted across Cait's face. She stood and patted Baird's hand across the table.

"Stick with her. You'll have your answers when you need them most," Cait said enigmatically and walked to the door.

"Right big help you are then," Baird shouted after her and she waved cheerfully back at him.

Baird finished his drink and stood, his thoughts in turmoil.

How did she know that he wasn't alone at the cove when it had lit up?

And what did that mean for him and Aislinn?

CHAPTER 30

"YOU SURE THAT you're okay?" Aislinn asked Morgan at the bottom of the stairs to her apartment.

Morgan nodded adamantly.

"I am, thank you." Impulsively she wrapped her arms around Aislinn and squeezed her quickly before buzzing out of the door with a quick, "See you Tuesday." Morgan worked Flynn's boat on Mondays, Thursdays and Fridays.

Pleased that Morgan had felt comfortable enough to hug her, Aislinn stepped out into her courtyard. Scanning the sky and seeing no hint of rain, she ran back upstairs and snagged the rest of the open bottle of wine and her glass. With a sketchpad tucked under her arm, she moved to her chair and small drafting table in a corner of the yard and set her pad up. She'd already considered doing a series of Ross Castle and the lake. The black swan stood out to her so adamantly that her fingers all but itched to draw it.

Aislinn tacked her paper to her board and began to lay in the outline of the water with the black swan. She'd probably replicate this sketch in oils at some point but she always liked to draw up her idea first.

Humming softly to herself, Aislinn lost herself in the mood of the evening, and the motion of her hand against the paper.

"Damn swan," Baird uttered from behind her and Aislinn shrieked and dropped her charcoal on the ground.

Putting her hand to her chest, she took a moment to turn, trying to calm her rapidly beating heart.

"Sure and you're trying to give me a heart attack?" Aislinn turned and smiled at Baird, realizing how happy she was to see him again.

That he had come back for her.

Baird moved closer and studied her work. "This is beautiful. You've true talent."

"Thank you," Aislinn murmured, smiling up at him.

"How's Morgan?"

"She's okay." Aislinn stood and crossed the courtyard to her table. "Wine?"

"Beer?" Baird asked.

"Sure," Aislinn said, suddenly feeling nervous, like a schoolgirl on her first date. She stepped inside and quickly ducked into the small bathroom on the first floor, groaning at her reflection in the mirror. She'd never bothered to put more makeup on after their spill in the lake and her hair was a riot of curls around her head. Her makeup was a lost cause but the hair could be fixed. She quickly twisted her curls into an intricate knot at the base of her neck.

Snagging two bottles of Harp from the fridge, Aislinn stepped back outside and saw Baird sitting comfortably on the picnic bench, back to the table, legs outstretched, staring up at the stars in the night sky.

"Nice night," he said as she approached and handed him a bottle.

"It is." Aislinn sat next to him and leaned back to look up at the stars. They winked down, icy diamonds against midnight blue, so sure of their place in the universe. Aislinn wondered where her place was and why she'd so recently felt like she'd lost her footing.

"Patrick?" Aislinn asked.

"Frustrated. He didn't do anything."

"I know," Aislinn said.

"What's Morgan's background?" Baird asked as he took a long pull from his bottle of beer.

"She's an orphan," Aislinn said. Baird nodded as if everything suddenly made perfect sense. And to him, perhaps it did.

"Patrick likes her," Baird said.

"Aye, she likes him too."

"What should we do about it?" Baird asked.

"Not a damn thing," Aislinn laughed over at him and then the smile dropped from her face. "Um, do you ever, like, do charity cases?"

Baird turned and looked at Aislinn, wrapping his arm around her back and pulling her closer to snuggle in the crook of his arm. Aislinn's insides warmed at his touch and she was surprised that for just a moment, she felt a little weepy. Just a little sentimental, Aislinn thought, and focused back on the conversation.

"You want me to talk to Morgan for free is what I'm getting here?"

Aislinn shrugged and looked back up at the sky.

"It wouldn't hurt. She doesn't trust many people. I'm not sure how much she would open up to you but I can certainly see that she has some scars to work on. But, maybe I'll take her off to Fiona instead."

"Ah, the great Fiona. I've yet to meet this mystery woman," Baird remarked. Aislinn drew back at the sting in his words. Was she misinterpreting him? Reaching out with her mind, she scanned him and realized that he was just a little bit angry.

"I'm sorry, but is there a problem here? Why are you mad at Fiona?"

"I'm not mad at Fiona," Baird said stiffly.

"At me, then," Aislinn said and drew fully away to turn on the bench and look at him. Baird's body was tense and his hand played a *tap-tap-tap* rhythm on his leg.

"I'm not angry at you," Baird said.

"You're lying," Aislinn said, not feeling the need to point out that she could read him a mile away. If the man didn't understand her gift by now, then she was done trying to explain it.

"Sure, and you'd know that. Just like Cait can pluck thoughts from my mind, and who knows what else everyone in this town can do. I'm starting to feel like I'm the target of some big game."

Aislinn's mouth dropped open and she felt her Irish kick up a notch. Or ten.

"Excuse me?" Aislinn said icily.

"You heard me. They're my feelings and I'm entitled to them. And right now? I feel like this whole town is in on some ruse."

Aislinn shoved herself off the bench and paced in front of him, trying to bring her temper down.

"Oh and what would this ruse be for? For sport? Let's all have a laugh at the new guy in town?" Aislinn said archly.

"Maybe it's just a ruse to the rest of the world. For tourism purposes. If the whole town is in on the act then people can come here and get a magickal experience. Good for the town. Actually, the more that I think about it, it makes perfect sense," Baird said heatedly and came to stand in front of her.

Aislinn's chest heaved as her brain whirled in frustration and anger.

Oh, so much anger.

She raised her chin and met Baird's gaze dead on.

"I have never been so insulted in my life. You think that I would start a personal relationship with someone and yet…lie about this?" She swept her hand out to encompass her back yard and then the town.

"Well, I don't know that, do I? Seems like everyone else is in the know on stuff and I'm not. I'd be the butt of the joke, wouldn't I?" Baird shouted at her and Aislinn stared at him in disbelief.

She felt like he'd punched her in the gut, her stomach suddenly queasy with anger.

"Get out," Aislinn whispered and pointed to the gate in her fence.

"Excuse me?" Baird asked, stepping closer so he towered over her.

"You don't scare me, Baird Delaney. I said…get out," Aislinn ordered, never breaking eye contact with him. He watched her and then cursed softly beneath his breath.

"I should have known you wouldn't stick this through," Baird hissed and stormed past her.

"And what's that supposed to mean?" Aislinn shouted at him, sincerely shocked at his statement.

"It means that girls that take guys home on the first night never stick in it when the relationship gets tough," Baird said and Aislinn's temper went through the roof.

"I know that you didn't just imply that I was the town hussy you arrogant, overbearing, hardheaded stump of a man," Aislinn shrieked after him.

"I don't know, Aislinn, why don't you just read how I'm feeling about you?" Baird shouted over the fence and slammed the gate door for good measure. He disappeared from her sight and Aislinn turned and huffed out a breath as she stormed her courtyard.

That *bastard*, she thought. Aislinn wasn't sure when she'd ever been more insulted.

The man had just called her a hussy. A lying one at that. He thought the whole town was out to get him? Like anyone had that much time on their hands! Aislinn muttered to herself as she paced her courtyard. Spying her glass of wine, she stormed back over and snagged the bottle, filling her glass to the rim.

She hurt.

Aislinn blinked back tears and swore that she would not cry over Baird. If she cried, then he had meant something more to her. And, it was clear that they weren't ever going to be a couple. Kicking a rock away with her foot, she crossed to where the candlelight flickered across the drawing of her swan.

The one place she could lose herself, no matter her emotions. With a sigh, she picked her charcoal up from the ground and sat, bringing her hand to the paper.

And began the process of removing Baird from her mind.

CHAPTER 31

"*O*H MY GOD," Morgan gasped as she stepped into the studio and found Aislinn at her desk, staring blearily into her cup of coffee.

"Hi, Morgan," Aislinn said softly.

"Aislinn, oh my, did you do all this? Since I left on Sunday?" Morgan asked, turning to stare at the back half of the gallery.

Canvases covered the walls. They leaned against the floor, were hung on any available hook, and more were lined up with space separating them so they could dry. The sea was found there. Angry, tempestuous waves raged across canvases, fighting their way out from the storm of the sea, making a person want to reach out and touch the water. Just for a second…to see if it was real.

"These are…wow, just wow. Amazing, so angry, so violent. God, Ash, I'm just in awe of your talent," Morgan breathed as she walked between them all.

"Thank you," Aislinn said softly.

"They are for the show?"

"Yes, I needed to get some of the seascapes done."

"Are you painting all the moods of the ocean?" Morgan asked, crossing her hands across her chest and biting her lip as she took in Aislinn's disheveled appearance.

"I suppose that you could say that," Aislinn said.

"Um, when did you eat last?"

Aislinn raised bloodshot eyes to Morgan and tried to think about when she had last eaten.

"I can't remember…" She squinted her eyebrows in confusion.

"Okay, not good. I'm going out for food. Stay," Morgan ordered and disappeared from the back door. Aislinn didn't have the heart to tell her that she probably wouldn't be able to stomach the food that the girl brought for her. She rose and went to stand in front of her work.

She'd been in a fury after Baird had left her. She'd found that she couldn't finish the drawing of the swan that she had started. It was a happy memory and it seemed wrong to draw it in anger. Instead, angry waves had crashed from her fingers and she'd been all but possessed as she had worked through the night, and into the next day.

Morgan was right, she thought. Her paintings were magnificent. Edgier than any she had done before. She nibbled at her thumbnail as she circled her entire shop, drawing her eyes over paintings of tranquil waters to sunshiny days to turbulent storms. Morgan was right about this as well, Aislinn thought. She was painting all the moods of the sea.

Like a messy, arrogant, and fiercely proud woman, the sea showcased her moods in any way that she could.

Aislinn was proud to honor the sea and to showcase the chameleon nature of her waters. Aislinn would never tire of watching the water that touched the shores of her small village or filled the enchanted cove.

Aislinn was fiercely proud of her work, of her village, and her lineage. She didn't think she'd realized that until Baird had insulted all of it. And had hurt her to the core.

Good riddance, she thought and took a deep breath as Morgan breezed back in the door with a bag from the café.

"More coffee, muffins, and some hardboiled eggs. I figured you may need some protein," Morgan said, eager to please.

"Thanks, Morgan," Aislinn said and moved to sit at her small table in the kitchenette. Morgan was silent as she unpacked the food but Aislinn could read her nervousness. Too tired to care about making Morgan feel better, she tore off a piece of a cranberry muffin and chewed mechanically.

"Um, so, is everything okay with you and Baird?" Morgan asked carefully.

Aislinn just raised an eyebrow at her and remained silent.

"I'm not trying to pry or anything. But, um, it's hard not to read you…you know, with my powers and all," Morgan said and blushed before quickly shoving a piece of muffin in her mouth to stem the flow of words.

"Lord save me from women with special abilities in my life," Aislinn said crankily and raised her eyebrows to the ceiling. She was rewarded with a peal of laughter from Morgan. Aislinn couldn't help but smile back since Morgan laughed so rarely.

"Why do you ask, Morgan?"

"It's just that, well, you can see it here," Morgan said and swept her hand to the works that lined the wall.

"I suppose you can tell that I've been a bit moody," Aislinn concurred.

Morgan barked out another laugh and Aislinn smiled again.

"A little? This is fury! Beautiful, stunning, fury," Morgan said.

Aislinn turned to study her work. She supposed that it was a tad bit angry.

"We'll call this my rage period," Aislinn said with a small smile as she blew on her coffee.

"I just…he didn't look too good, either," Morgan said hesitantly and Aislinn's head snapped up as she scanned Morgan's face.

"You saw him?"

"Um, yes?" Morgan's voice went up in a "is that a bad thing if I did?" note.

"Like at the market?"

"No, he stopped by the docks and invited me for a free session," Morgan said softly and cast her eyes down at the table. Aislinn's mouth dropped open and for some reason she became even angrier. Damn that man for going and doing something sweet right in the middle of her hating him.

"I'm sorry, please don't be mad," Morgan said, correctly interpreting Aislinn's reaction.

"I'm not mad at you at all," Aislinn said, waving away Morgan's concerns easily.

"It was nice," Morgan said nervously and Aislinn pulled her mind away from herself for a moment.

"You talked to him then? How do you feel about it?"

Morgan tore apart her muffin on her plate as she thought about her response.

"I feel like it would be good for me to go a few more times. I'm...I'm not quite comfortable with how much I can tell him, yet. Not sure if I trust him with all of it," Morgan said and made a circle motion with her finger to point at her mind. Aislinn knew that she was referencing her gift.

"I know what I'd like you to do, but that would be out of spite," Aislinn murmured.

"What's that?"

"I'd love for you to make something fly across the room. To show him straight out your power so he doesn't believe the whole town is lying to him," Aislinn grumbled. Morgan gaped at her.

"You told him about your power?"

"Aye, I'm honest about it. At least to those that I feel comfortable with."

"And he thinks you're lying?" Morgan raised her eyebrows.

"He does. In fact, he seems to think the whole town is in on some big lie to attract tourists." Aislinn shoved away from the table to pace again. Just thinking about it made her start to get angry all over again.

"Well...that's the dumbest thing that I've ever heard," Morgan decided. "Which is weird...'cause the doc seems like a pretty smart guy."

"Oh, he is. Smart, sensitive, and..." Aislinn trailed off

as she realized that she was about to gush over him. Shaking it off, she turned to face Morgan.

"I'll stop going to him. That jerk," Morgan decided.

"No. Please, go. If you can get free counseling, then take it," Aislinn urged. "Don't let my personal relationship step in the way of you learning to heal some of your wounds, okay?"

"If you're sure."

"Yes, please. It's really important to learn to let go of old baggage. This will be good for you. And, you're going to want to feel better about dating Patrick."

Morgan hunched over and crossed her arms, tearing apart her already mangled muffin.

"He left flowers for me at my van," Morgan whispered. Crumbs went flying as she picked apart the muffin.

"Morgan. Stop," Aislinn said and the girl jumped and looked down at her destroyed muffin.

"Oh, jeez. Sorry," Morgan said.

"It's fine. They're your muffins to destroy. But, I meant stop closing in on yourself when a cute boy likes you. I can tell you that Patrick is a standup guy, okay?"

"He is?" Hope flitted across Morgan's face.

"He is. But, make him work for it," Aislinn cautioned.

Morgan nodded furiously and Aislinn sighed at the eagerness in her face. Did she look like that when she thought about Baird? Ugh, Aislinn thought and moved to put her dish in the sink.

"So, he looked rough?" Aislinn could kick herself for asking.

"Yes, he had dark circles under his eyes. He was thinking about you. As soon as he saw me, his thoughts went to you. I don't know, Ash. He's pretty torn up. I think he really cares about you," Morgan said hesitantly.

Aislinn shrugged her shoulders.

"Well, he doesn't show it very well now, does he?"

Morgan opened her mouth but Aislinn held up her hand to silence her.

"Come, help me catalog these paintings. I need to take pictures of them and note their dimensions to send to the gallery in Dublin," Aislinn said and Morgan hopped up, all business.

"Can I come to your show? Will you need help?" Morgan asked breathlessly.

Aislinn stopped. She hadn't even thought about inviting anyone yet or how she would get all the work there.

"I have a van," Morgan offered, reading her mind.

"Yes, I'd love for you to come to the show with me and be my assistant. I'll pay you, of course," Aislinn said automatically.

Morgan squealed and clapped her hands, looking like a dark-haired fairy as she flitted around the room chattering about the show. Aislinn followed her movements and silently counted all her paintings as Morgan talked. She'd need at least a dozen more before next week.

Her heart skipped a beat.

Her show was in just over a week.

Forcing herself to breathe, she marched around the room and began to make mental notes of all the different moods of a woman and how the sea resembled them. As the idea took shape in her mind, she began to see her other paintings. She had anger, gentleness, sadness, and happiness. What was she missing?

Love, she thought bitterly and turned away from her work.

"Morgan, I'm going up for a quick nap. I need to work through pretty much the next two weeks. How much time can you be here?"

"I'll ask Flynn if I can have the next two weeks off."

"Thank you," Aislinn said wearily and climbed the stairs to her apartment. She stepped into her room and dropped face first onto her bed. Her mind whirling with images of the sea in all its moods, she fell off the edge into a dreamless sleep.

CHAPTER 32

*B*AIRD STOOD AT his window and watched as Morgan approached his office. It had been several days since their first appointment and he was glad that she had decided to come back to talk with him again. He sensed that there was a lot of underlying anger and insecurity that she needed to deal with. Baird didn't even care that she couldn't pay. In some ways, he needed to help her. For Aislinn.

Maybe for himself, Baird thought with a shrug. If treating Morgan for free was some way to atone for hurting Aislinn then he had a pretty messed up way of apologizing, the psychiatrist inside of him lectured.

Yeah, yeah, Baird thought. I know what I'm doing.

He needed to go see Aislinn. He'd found himself unconsciously thinking about her through the week, wanting to ring her when something funny crossed his mind or when he saw something that he knew she would want to paint or photograph. It was like she had opened his eyes to the world and Baird found himself stopping in his everyday routine and looking around him, seeing the beauty in the everyday.

Was the village really in on some big hoax? The more he met and interacted with the locals, the harder he found it to believe.

And, yet, he still needed answers.

A part of him hated that he did. Why couldn't he just let it go and accept what was? He could've kicked himself the other night for saying the things he did. It was like they had just rolled off his tongue of their own accord.

Baird trotted down the stairs to his office at the knock on his door.

"Hi, Morgan." Baird held the door open for the girl and was relieved to see her smile up at him.

"Hi, Dr. Delaney," Morgan said shyly.

"You can call me Baird," he said with a smile. They'd pretty much moved past formalities when he'd interrupted that little scene between her and Patrick last week. He gestured for her to sit on his couch and took a club-style chair across from her. Sensing that she wasn't a fan of protocol, Baird kept his notebook down and instead moved to a small refrigerator.

"Water?"

"Sure, thanks," she said.

Morgan crossed her legs and pulled a pillow onto her lap. A wall.

Protection, Baird thought.

"How have things been since our first session?" Baird began.

Morgan shrugged her shoulder.

"Good, I guess. I've been busy."

"Work?"

"Yes, helping Aislinn get ready for her show. She's painting like she's possessed," Morgan said, her eyes trained on his face.

"I'm sure. She's very talented," Baird said.

"In more ways than one," Morgan said, meaning behind her voice.

Baird met her eyes but didn't say anything. It would violate Aislinn's confidentiality to discuss her gift with Morgan, irrespective of whether the girl knew about it.

"How do you like working for her?" Baird asked instead.

"I love it. I find her to be so inspiring. She's the first person, aside from Flynn, that's really given me a chance. I'm learning so much," Morgan gushed.

"You didn't have a lot of chances...or choices... growing up, did you?"

Morgan's shoulders instantly slumped.

"No, not many choices. Until I made the one to leave."

"Tell me about why you ran away, if you can," Baird asked.

Morgan watched Baird for a moment before reaching for her water bottle. Not saying a word, she set it back down on the table. She looked at the water bottle and back at Baird as he waited patiently for her to begin her story.

"I shouldn't say that I didn't have choices. I had power. Which gives me certain options that others don't have," Morgan said softly.

Baird raised an eyebrow at her but held himself back from a laugh. Another one with power? Right, he thought sarcastically to himself.

Anger flashed across Morgan's beautiful face and his mouth dropped open as her water bottle flew into the air, hovered over his head, before dumping the contents in his lap.

"Hey!" Baird shouted, gasping in shock as he stared at Morgan, his mind working furiously to resolve what had just happened.

Morgan jumped up and met his shout with her own.

"Hey back! I can hear what you're thinking! I don't need you to condescend to me with your stupid smile and biased thoughts. I can HEAR YOU. Do you get that? I've always had these powers. Nobody has ever understood me. I've had nobody to help me. My whole life." Angry tears sprang into Morgan's gorgeous eyes, "Not until I came here. For the first time in my life, I've found people who accept me. As I am. And, Dr. Delaney, I don't need you or anyone else to pass your judgment."

Morgan's thin body trembled with her anger and surprise crossed her face at her words. Baird gathered that she didn't shout that often. She turned to go.

"Sit, please," Baird said, shaking his head at what had just transpired. He was used to patients acting out, but this was a whole new level. What was it with this town? There was no way that he could deny what he had just seen. Baird closed his eyes for a moment and sighed.

He owed Aislinn an apology.

Morgan sat and crossed her arms, angrily wiping away the tears that continued to spring into her eyes.

"I'm sorry," she whispered softly, refusing to look at the water spot that stained his trousers.

Baird walked over to the side table and picked up a

napkin to dab at his pants. So, Morgan seemed to have more than one gift. He'd have to be careful around her.

"I won't hurt you," Morgan said, clearly offended.

Baird turned and surprised himself by laughing at her.

"I know. I meant careful in my thoughts. As a psychiatrist, I have to run through a few possibilities for what may be going on with you in my head. If you can hear my thoughts, you can't jump to any conclusions. You're going to have to let me be your doctor or I can't treat you."

Morgan's mouth dropped open.

"You'd still want to treat me?"

"Of course. You still want help, don't you?"

Morgan nodded her head vigorously.

"Please," she whispered. "Please don't give up on me."

Baird walked over and held out his hand to her.

"You stay out of my mind and let me work on helping you and promise not to pull any more tricks and I'll treat you. Deal?"

Morgan's hand felt warm and clammy in his own, and he was suddenly grateful that he had the opportunity to treat her. It was clear that healing herself was very important to her.

"Deal," Morgan whispered.

CHAPTER 33

*A*ISLINN STOOD BACK and studied the vision that had come to her during a dream one night. It would be the masterpiece, the showpiece, the grand dame of the collection, she thought.

It was a triptych. A three-paneled painting of the ocean. Each canvas would be framed in driftwood and was floor-to-ceiling height. She'd had to lay the canvas on the floor of her apartment to paint and then alternate between getting a ladder and tacking them to the wall to stand before them and see the paintings from that angle.

It was all the moods of the sea in one. The water rolled between the three panels, from softly gentle waters to a raging fury in the last piece.

But it was the middle piece that haunted her.

The cove jutted out, proudly arrogant, owning the middle panel, showcasing how land and sea warred with each other.

Loved each other.

But, she wasn't finished. Wasn't sure if she could finish

it. If she could really feel what was needed in order to complete it.

Aislinn brought her hands to her eyes in balled fists. When she closed her eyes she could all but feel how the painting should be finished, but something stopped her from bringing the image out of her mind. Into her work.

It was enough to drive her mad. Or make her cry. Instead, she moved into her kitchen for a sip of whiskey. She'd bypassed wine earlier this week and instead went straight for the hard stuff to take the edge off the emotions that raged inside of her when she painted. Whomever said painting was cathartic was nuts, Aislinn thought. It was more like opening a wound and then pouring salt in it, she thought as she laughed into her glass of whiskey.

A knock at her back door had her head lifting up. Aislinn glanced to the clock by her bed. It was after 11:00 at night.

Baird.

A part of her had known that he would come. Just as she knew that she was powerless to ignore his knock. Putting her whiskey down, she pushed her hair back and padded softly down the stairs to the door, where she could see his face framed in the light on the back stoop. She stood for a moment, not letting him in, watching him through the glass.

In his eyes was a question.

One that she knew she would have to answer.

Aislinn opened the door and remained silent, tilting her head to look up at him.

Baird bent and wrapped his arms around her, crushing her lips in a kiss that burned straight to her soul. She could have sworn that she heard trumpets or some type of epic music in her head as he swooped her up and carried her up the stairs, his lips never leaving hers.

Aislinn's heart clenched as he walked backwards with her into the room. God, she'd wanted him. Ached for him. She hadn't wanted to believe it was over and yet couldn't understand why he had left her. Hadn't trusted her.

Baird broke his lips away from hers, his chest heaving as he struggled to catch his breath and he brought his eyes up, past hers, to the painting behind her.

Aislinn gasped as he looked back down at her. Baird's eyes were so full of passion...of love...that it made her heart sing. Reaching out, she felt his emotions wash over her and she wanted to weep in joy. There was nothing but lust and love.

Baird loved her.

He didn't have to say it, Aislinn could feel it. Aislinn reached up and pressed her hand to his cheek, tears clouding her eyes. She hadn't known that this was what she had really wanted until it had happened. It was easier to convince herself that she didn't care. A moan escaped her mouth as he lowered her to the floor in front of her painting.

Without a word, he began to love her. It was his own way of telling her how he felt. His hands traced up her bare legs to where her ragged sleep shorts barely covered her. She shivered as he caressed her inner thighs, running his hands up beneath her shorts to caress the line of her underwear.

Hadn't he wanted to wait? What had happened? Why now?

Aislinn gasped as he ran a finger beneath her underwear and tugged slightly. Lifting her hips, she allowed him
to tug the shorts from her legs.

Baird paused between her legs to look down at her. She
knew that her hair was a mess and that paint was probably
all over the thin tank that she wore. Personal appearance
mattered little to her when she painted.

For a second, everything stopped. The world narrowed
to a little pinpoint. Warm light from her table lamp slashed
across Baird's face and Aislinn could see the colors of her
paintings behind him, the war and fury of the ocean raging
around his body. It all melded together in harmony with
his emotions and Aislinn's body sang as he knelt and thrust
inside of her in one smooth motion.

Her head fell back against the hard floor and she didn't
care that it was uncomfortable or that they were half-
dressed. It felt so right, so raw, that her body seemed to
throb around Baird's as he stroked deep inside of her,
cradling her in his arms as he pushed her to the point of
madness…into ecstasy. Aislinn sobbed into his mouth as
he pulled her deeper down through the emotional layers
and more into love than she'd ever been with anyone else
before.

Their lips mingled, their bodies moving together as
one, as Baird brought her, trembling, to the precipice of a
love so sweet, so open, that her body ached with wanting
it. On a moan, she shattered around him and swallowed his
cries of lust with her mouth, never wanting to leave this
moment.

Spent, Baird rolled and pulled her on top of him, cush-
ioning her from the hard floor. Aislinn brushed her hair

back from her face and pillowed her arms on his chest, looking down into his silver eyes.

"I missed you," Baird said simply.

"I see that," Aislinn said, laughing down at his face.

"I'm sorry, Ash. I shouldn't have said…the things that I did," he whispered and Aislinn could feel the real pain in his voice.

"That's okay. You're a man. Men have a tendency to be idiots at times in their lives," Aislinn said magnanimously.

Baird raised his eyebrow at her. "Did you just call me an idiot after I made love to you?"

Aislinn grinned down at him. "Oh, was that love you were making?"

Baird reached up and traced a hand down her cheek, over her nose and down her bottom lip.

"Aye, it was. I love you, Ash. I don't know why or how, or fully understand you, but you're all that I can think about. It's not just lust, I know the difference," Baird said.

"Well sure and I thought that I'd seduced you into lust," Aislinn teased.

"I thought that too," Baird said seriously and Aislinn jokingly smacked him in the head.

"That's why you were all about being hands off?"

"I just felt like I wanted to know you better. It didn't make sense to me that I would feel so much…so quickly." Baird shrugged.

Aislinn tilted her head and looked down at him.

"Don't you believe in love at first sight, Doctor?"

"No, I don't. Or, I didn't, I guess," Baird said, scrunching his nose up as he thought about it.

"Not everything lines up neatly like in those textbooks of yours, does it?" Aislinn asked quietly.

"No," Baird admitted, watching her. "But, human emotion is messy and often doesn't follow textbooks. Even I know that."

"What about the other stuff? My gift?"

"I love you and that is part of you so I can accept that."

Something about the way he said it rankled, like he was giving her a gift or something. Aislinn, for the first time in her life, decided to keep her mouth shut and not ruin the moment. Especially when she could tell what he was feeling. There was no animosity behind his words.

"I guess I'll have to learn to accept that you are some fancy doctor then," Aislinn said instead and was rewarded with a laugh from Baird. Aislinn giggled as her stomach growled loudly on Baird and he looked at her in awe.

"Not eating much?"

"Between being angry at you and having to get ready for my show, food kind of falls off my radar," Aislinn admitted.

"Let me feed you," Baird said and moved to sit up.

Aislinn rolled from him and stopped when she saw Baird frozen, staring at her canvases.

"These…they're stunning. Almost painfully so. My God, Ash. You take my breath away."

Baird went and stood before the panels and Aislinn had the distinct pleasure of admiring his naked rear end. Maybe that was the missing part to her middle part of the painting, she mused. A snicker escaped her and Baird turned to narrow his eyes at her.

"Sorry, I was thinking about painting you into my canvas. Just like that." Aislinn gestured.

"Oh yeah? How's this?" Baird bent his knees and pushed his butt out like he was a girl and Aislinn fell over herself laughing.

"Don't get mad if something like that appears in my show," she called after his retreating back end.

Aislinn snagged her sleep shorts and pulled them over her legs and stood in front of her painting. She closed her eyes and could feel what she needed to do. She was dying to pick up her brush, but knew that sometimes the artist in her had to wait.

"I've got the dinner of champions starting in here," Baird called from the kitchen. He poked his head out to her. "Grilled cheese and soup sound good?"

"Perfect." Aislinn grinned at him, feeling giddy at the turn her night had taken.

Glad that she hadn't overthought it. That she'd let him in.

Grateful that she had allowed emotions to rule her world instead of pride.

"Get comfortable, I'll serve you," Baird called from the kitchen and Aislinn raised her eyebrows at that. A man who cooked and served the food? Smiling, she made quick use of the bathroom and then padded over to her low-slung couch, pulling a throw over her bare legs.

Baird came out of the kitchen carrying two plates with cups of soup and sandwiches on them.

"Triangles?" Aislinn asked, raising her eyebrow at the neatly cut sandwich.

"Always," Baird said and sat next to her, stretching his

legs so that their feet intertwined on the couch. Steam poured from the top of the mug and Aislinn blew on it as she looked at him over the rim. He looked rumpled and comfortable on her couch, at ease with the world and himself.

How had they gotten here? From in a fury a week ago to comfortably cozying up on the couch over soup and a sandwich.

She'd opened the door for him, hadn't she?

"What made you come here tonight?" Aislinn asked, taking a bite of her grilled cheese sandwich, crisped to perfection.

Baird shrugged his shoulders and sipped at his soup, looking over at her wall of paintings.

"Morgan came to see me."

Aislinn didn't say anything, waiting him out. He raised his eyebrow at her and laughed.

"Aye, so you know the power of silence in getting someone to talk then?"

Aislinn smiled at him cheerfully and a laugh bubbled from him, low and long. She wanted to crawl across the couch and snuggle up on his muscular chest.

"I can't talk about our sessions, as it is privileged infor-mation. Needless to say, she's opened my eyes to a few things."

"Like the fact that extra abilities are a very real thing?" Aislinn asked archly.

Baird sighed and ran his hand through his thick hair. "Listen, it's not that I doubted you. Okay, maybe it is…" He held up his hand to silence her when she tried to speak. "It's that it was weird for me to go from never being around someone with extra abilities to suddenly having a whole town seemingly comfortable with all this... magickal stuff."

"That you know of..." Aislinn said.

"What's that?"

"You've never spent time around someone with extra power *that you know of*," Aislinn clarified.

Baird looked astounded at that realization and Aislinn choked out a laugh. She suspected that she would continue to rock Baird's narrow world view for quite a while yet.

"I just...don't you want to know why? Magick doesn't make sense to me. Science does. I'm sorry that I am this way, but I just automatically seek answers. To explain." Baird held up his hands beseechingly and Aislinn sighed at his words.

"And if there are no explanations? Other than what we've been told?"

"Then I have to accept it. Magick."

"Why can't you just accept that now?" Aislinn asked, bitterness seeping into her tone.

"Ash, this is all new to me. I can't help that my mind immediately jumps to wanting to figure it out. To study it." Baird shrugged his shoulders, looking confused and shaken.

"So what does that mean for us?"

"I know that I want to be with you," Baird said simply.

"And that's it? What about the future?"

Tilting his head, Baird studied her from behind his glasses, his silver eyes bright with intelligence and love.

"I say that we deepen our bond a day at a time and the future will plan itself."

Aislinn's mouth dropped open. It was the most "by the seat of the pants" statement that she had heard from the uptight doctor yet.

"So, no boundaries or rules? Or are we in a relationship?"

Baird looked deeply offended. "Of course we are in a relationship. I don't cheat and I don't lie. I am going to be honest with people if they ask if I'm dating you."

Warmth spread through Aislinn's chest and she toasted Baird with her grilled cheese in her hand.

"Dating it is. I like the sound of that," Aislinn agreed and smiled across at him, her mouth full of sandwich and heart full of love.

"Now, get out," Aislinn said and pointed towards the door. Baird's mouth dropped open.

"You've got to be kidding me."

Shaking her head, Aislinn put her empty plate down on the table in front of the couch. "I'm sorry, but I have to keep working."

"Through the night?" Baird asked in disbelief.

Shrugging her shoulders, Aislinn nodded. "I have to finish this grand piece. And, I have several more paintings to go. Not only do they need to be finished, but they have to dry, be framed, and get packed up before the end of the week."

Leaning back, Baird crossed his arms behind his neck.

"Can't I watch you paint?"

"You most certainly cannot," Aislinn replied immediately.

"Ah, artistic temperament, I see." Baird's lips quirked at her.

Aislinn raised her nose at him. "Something like that."

"I'll go, on one, no, two conditions."

"What's that?"

"Come over here for a kiss," Baird said.

Aislinn put her hands on her hips and waited. "And the other?"

"Come here and find out."

Aislinn giggled at him and crawled across the couch, landing on his chest hard enough to make him go "ooof." She buried her nose in his neck, inhaling the clean scent of him and all but arched her back when his arms came around her to hold her tight to him. Looking up, she raised her head enough to nip at his bottom lip.

"The second condition?"

"That wasn't much of a kiss," Baird said.

Aislinn arched back and, supporting herself on his shoulders, she leaned in and kissed him, pouring all of her love and angst into it, until their lips were hot and they both gasped for breath.

"The second?" Aislinn asked again.

"I want to come to your show. As your date," Baird asked.

Aislinn smiled against his mouth.

"I'd like that."

CHAPTER 34

*T*HE DAYS BEFORE her show passed in a blur of painting, making love with Baird and then unceremoniously kicking him out afterwards, and a detailed level of organization skills that she wasn't used to employing.

She couldn't have been happier.

Aislinn hummed as she cut driftwood pieces with a small power saw in her back courtyard. Today she was framing up her main showpiece. Whistling, she lined the lengths of driftwood to her measurements on the ground. Standing above them, she examined each piece with a critical eye. Turning one another direction and removing another and replacing it with a knottier piece, she finally nodded her approval. With small wood nails, she deftly nailed each of the corners together, allowing the natural ends to stick out in uneven shapes. After she affixed the driftwood to the stretched canvas frames, she would cover the nail marks with corded leather, wrapping the cord around the ends and knotting it.

Aislinn hefted the first frame over her head and marched inside, up to her apartment. No one had seen these three paintings yet. Well, aside from Baird, she thought. Even then, she'd covered the finished product after the first night that he had come to see her.

That night.

Aislinn flashed back to their raw, yet achingly beautiful, sex on the floor in front of her paintings. She had never wanted someone to stay as much as she had wanted him to go before. Her hands had been itching to complete the painting and it had taken all of her willpower to sit and eat with him.

When he'd gone, finally, Aislinn had run upstairs and dove for her paints. She'd stood in front of the middle canvas, the one depicting the cove, and had closed her eyes for a moment. She could see the painting in her mind's eye, pulsing with color and emotion. Opening her eyes, she'd narrowed in on the waters of the cove and had begun to paint.

Aislinn smiled now as she held the frame to the middle painting. It was perfect. Her brow broke out in a sweat and her heart raced as she stepped back from the three paintings. What does one do when confronted with what might possibly be their best work? She tried to calm her breath as she allowed her love for these panels to flow through her. Selling them just might break her heart.

"Ash?" Morgan called to her from downstairs.

"Coming!" Aislinn called, not wanting Morgan to come up and see her paintings. She laughed a little at herself as she descended the stairs. In a matter of days, the entire city of Dublin could see her work if they so chose.

Aislinn bounced into her store, running on energy and love.

"Fiona!"

Aislinn beamed as the elder woman stood in front of one of her paintings, shaking her head. Today Fiona was outfitted in a light woven dress that reached to her ankles and swirled in a bright fuchsia and maroon pattern. Her hair was tied back with twine, and bracelets with varying stones crowded her wrists. They jangled as she held her arms up for a hug from Aislinn. Aislinn held on a little longer than usual. Hugging Fiona was like coming home, and it calmed her jittery nerves.

She caught Morgan nervously hanging around the edge of the room and motioned for the girl to come over.

"Morgan, this is the great Fiona that I've told you about. Fiona, Morgan. I've been meaning to bring her to you."

"Is that so?" Fiona asked, her bright eyes crinkling at the corners as she turned to measure Morgan.

Morgan smiled shyly and held out her hand to Fiona, who took it and held it between both her hands. She nodded briskly at Morgan.

"You'll come to see me, then."

"Um, I will?" Morgan asked, uncertain of what Fiona was asking.

"Well? Don't you want to learn more about your power? Or powers, should I say?"

Aislinn cracked a smile as Morgan's mouth dropped open. People were never prepared for Fiona's honesty. But those with extra abilities? They were used to being the ones to surprise others. Rarely did someone surprise them with their own knowledge and power.

"Um, yeah, I guess. I mean, I don't know what there is to learn really..." Morgan's hands fluttered in front of her nervously.

Fiona smiled brightly at her and reached up to pat Morgan on the arm.

"That's the point of learning, isn't it? You don't know what more you can do until you try."

Aislinn laughed at Fiona and bent to kiss her cheek.

"Inarguable wisdom as usual."

"I heard your show is this week. I can't believe that you didn't invite me," Fiona said, censure ringing through her tone as she swept through the store.

"I didn't know you would want to come!" Aislinn said, honestly surprised.

Fiona turned her steely gaze on Aislinn.

"And why wouldn't I come to support one of my own?"

Warmth flooded Aislinn and she was surprised to feel a little lump form in her throat. She dug her toe into the ground, like a sheepish teenager being scolded.

"I don't know. It's a fair way to travel, I guess."

"I'm taking the train. I've already booked my hotel," Fiona said over her shoulder and turned to look at the canvases lining the walls.

"This one is one of my favorites," Morgan whispered and pointed to one of Aislinn's ocean of fury paintings. Fiona studied it for a while before turning to look at Aislinn.

"You've improved. Considerably. So, you're in love then?"

Aislinn swore that she could feel her cheeks heat.

"Nosy old woman, aren't you?"

Fiona broke into laughter that shook her thin shoulders before sweeping around the room to look at the rest of her work.

"Your show is going to be a smashing success," Fiona decided, circling back to Aislinn.

"Thank you, Fiona," Aislinn whispered, surprised to find that she had wanted Fiona's approval. Maybe even needed it.

"Okay, put me to work then," Fiona declared and turned to Morgan with her eyebrow raised. The girl sprang into action, showing Fiona where they were in the packaging and framing process.

"I'll wrap the finished products and document the list. You finish the frames," Fiona decided.

"Thanks, Fiona," Aislinn said with a smile and bent to grab a roll of the thick paper that would protect her three canvases upstairs. "I've got to finish a project upstairs. I'll be down in a bit."

Fiona turned and Aislinn swore that the old woman was going to insist on coming upstairs to look at her paintings. Instead, she only nodded at Aislinn and began to pepper Morgan with questions. Smiling, Aislinn raced upstairs and began work on the final driftwood frames for her panels.

An hour later, she had just finished wrapping the leather cord around the corners of the frames and pulling the protective sheeting over the large panels when she heard voices downstairs. She'd closed the shop for the rest of the week as there was no way she'd have the time or patience to deal with customers. Hearing Keelin's voice, she paused with her wrapping.

"Aislinn! We're coming up!"

Aislinn swung around to check that her paintings were totally covered and then shook her head at herself. If she was going to be so secretive about her work then why was she even showing them? Maybe she should just keep them for herself. A permanent exhibition of her most inspired work, she mused.

Keelin and Cait all but bounced into the room on a rush of enthusiasm and energy.

"We can't wait for your show!" Keelin crowed, her arms full of shopping bags. Cait followed at a slightly more sedate pace, her arms also full of bags.

"What's all this?" Aislinn asked, gesturing to the bags.

"Outfits!" Keelin sang out.

The blood all but drained from her face.

She'd forgotten to pick an outfit for her show. What had she been thinking? Aislinn rushed over and grabbed Cait, kissing her cheeks enthusiastically before grabbing Keelin and pulling her into an awkward three-person hug.

"I'd forgotten to pick an outfit!" Aislinn exclaimed.

"We figured as much. To the rescue we have come," Cait said with a smile and moved to plop down on the couch. She waved her hand at the large paintings in the corner. "For the show?"

"Yes, my main piece. Nobody's seen it. Well..." Aislinn trailed off.

Cait leaned forward and pounced.

"You and Baird did the dirty! Right here!"

Keelin squealed and grabbed Aislinn's arm, pulling her, shopping bags and all, to the couch. "Tell us everything."

Aislinn glared over at Cait. "Why don't you just ask Cait?"

Cait smiled sweetly at Aislinn. "I'm pregnant. You can't be mad at me. Hormones make me do impulsive things. Like read your mind and find out that you and Dr. Yum had some fun right here on the floor. And that he loves you."

Keelin gasped. "Oh, he loves you! Do you love him? What happened?"

Aislinn glared at Cait. "Why don't you just tell her, Cait?"

Cait held up her hands in defeat. "I don't know everything, not for lack of trying. I could read it in his mind the other night when he came to the pub."

Interested, Aislinn leaned back. "When was this?"

"The night he and Patrick had a pint."

Aislinn raised her eyebrows at Cait. "Then? You're sure? We had a huge fight that night."

Cait shrugged her shoulders. "The worst fights that I've had have been with the man that I love."

Keelin nodded solemnly. "It's true. Myself as well."

"Well, long story short, he's decided to accept my abilities, though he still seeks answers about them, and came over to tell me he loves me."

Keelin leaned back and looked at her. "What do you mean he still seeks answers?"

"Dr. Yum is a skeptic, Keelin," Cait said.

"Oh, so, what does that mean for you?" Keelin said, a worried line creasing her brow.

"It means that I just have to accept that he has the insatiable need for answers and once he finds out that there is no science behind our extra abilities, he'll have to calm down." Aislinn shrugged her shoulders as Keelin turned a steely gaze on Cait. A look passed between the two and Aislinn held up her hand to stop them.

"Look. We're dating. Exclusively. That's it."

"Have you told him that you love him?" Cait asked.

"Of course…" Aislinn stopped. Had she? "Um, actually, I don't think that I have."

"Good. It gives you leverage." Cait nodded her approval and Keelin frowned at her.

"Don't you think that you should tell him?"

"I'm sure that he knows. But I will. I can't believe that I didn't say it to him," Aislinn murmured.

The bags made a crackling sound as Cait dug in them and pulled out a bright red sheath. "This is a great dress. Go on, try it on."

Keelin clapped her hands. "Yes, model for us. Dress up time!"

Aislinn laughed, grateful for the both of them. She really couldn't believe that she had forgotten about what she was going to wear.

Aislinn took an hour to model for her friends, pawing through dresses, pants, and accessories and dancing around the room, pretending to be a snobby artist for the girls.

"Okay, I think we have a final two choices, yes?" Cait asked.

"Yes," Keelin said.

The first option was the deep red sheath that hugged her body like a second skin and made her look like a flame. She had a silver chain link bib-necklace that was perfect for the ensemble and if she left her hair in a riot of curls, she would give off a wild, yet sensual look.

The other option was a deep purple dress that had bright red accents at the trim and collar. It fell in a column straight to the floor and was made of thousands of tiny beads that moved with her body as she walked. For this, she'd pull back her hair and let the dress speak for itself.

"I like the red," Cait decided.

"I don't know. They are both great," Aislinn said.

"I don't want to look like a small-town artist. I want to look edgy and sexy," Aislinn decided.

The girls looked at each other before both turning to Aislinn and chorusing, "Red!"

"The purple really is great though," Keelin amended, running her fingers over the dress. "All that beadwork."

"I'll bring both and decide the day of," Aislinn decided. "Thank you so much for bringing these dresses for me. I don't know what I would have thrown on at the last minute if you two hadn't remembered!"

"We can't wait to see the show," Cait said.

"You're coming?" Aislinn asked, surprise evident in her voice.

"Sure and you don't think that we would miss your big debut show?" Keelin asked, aghast.

Aislinn shrugged her shoulders. "I guess, I just didn't expect people to travel all that way for my work. I mean, they can see it all right in my store."

"But not like we can see it at a big fancy gallery in Dublin now, can we?" Cait asked.

"We are so proud of you," Keelin followed up.

"Thanks, ladies. I'm so glad you came today. I needed this. I don't think that I realized how much I needed all of this support. Fiona, too."

"You're family," Keelin said simply and they crowded around Aislinn to give their well wishes before they clattered down the steps, chattering about what they were going to wear in Dublin.

Aislinn shook her head in surprise at herself. Sometimes she was so caught up in her art and managing her shop and her life on her own that she forgot to look to her support system. It had been stupid of her not to invite everyone to the show. She should've known that they would come anyway.

It felt good knowing people had her back.

Stretching, she walked to her paintings and finished with the final tape up.

"Morgan? Can you come help me?"

Together, they brought the wrapped canvases down to the main floor. Aislinn turned and surveyed the rows of wrapped paintings, amazed at how much she had produced in such a short time.

"I'll be ready with my van first thing in the morning," Morgan promised.

"Thanks, Morgan. Um, Baird wants to drive up with us, but he may take his own car."

"Go with him. I'll follow right behind you." Morgan waved a hand at her.

"Are you sure? That's a long drive on your own."

"I'm used to being alone," Morgan said and slipped out of the back door.

Aislinn understood that. She was used to being on her own and doing stuff for herself. But it was nice, wasn't it, to know that people were there when she needed it most? Smiling, she shut the lights off in her shop and hightailed it upstairs. She still needed to pack for the weekend.

CHAPTER 35

*A*ISLINN BARELY SLEPT a wink.

On her third cup of coffee, she grunted out orders as Morgan arrived at the shop, right on time.

"We need to do this by size," Aislinn said, desperately wishing that she had let Baird come over the night before. He probably would have calmed her enough to sleep. Or kept her mind off the show with other activities. Instead, she'd pushed him away, assuring him that she needed to sleep.

Ha, she thought.

Aislinn brought her hand to the back of her neck to work out a tense muscle as she surveyed her canvases, trying to determine which way to start.

"Good morning," Baird's voice called through the back door.

"We're in the shop," Aislinn called and then stopped when Baird rounded the corner with his hands full of bright red poppies.

Poppies.

Who would even think to pick that flower? It was one of her favorites, as she loved the bright red of the flowers juxtaposed against the green of the landscape. They'd always been a favorite of hers to paint. She didn't even know where one could get poppies in the small town of Grace's Cove.

"For my famous artist girlfriend." Baird smiled at her, handing her the bouquet. She swore that part of her wanted to squeal like a teenaged girl at him calling her his girlfriend, so she buried her face in the flowers before bringing her hand up to touch his cheek. Baird leaned down to brush his lips over hers, lingering for a moment.

"Thank you," Aislinn breathed against his mouth.

"Enough kissing, let's load up." Patrick's voice startled her and Aislinn craned her neck around Baird's arm to see Patrick standing in the back door, a broad smile stretching his handsome face.

Morgan immediately turned her back and began to shuffle through the canvases.

"Patrick! What are you doing here?"

"I'm here to help, Aislinn. I'm coming to the show if you don't mind." Patrick's words were for Aislinn but his eyes tracked Morgan.

Aislinn leaned back and met Baird's eyes.

"Let them work it out," he breathed against her lips.

"Sounds great, Patrick. We are just going to step upstairs so Baird can help me with my luggage," Aislinn decided on the spot and pulled Baird's hand to drag him past a smiling Patrick up the stairs to her apartment.

Once there, she gasped as Baird lifted her and swung her around the room, planting kisses all over her face.

"You look tired. Trouble sleeping?"

"Aye. I should have had you come over. I'm sorry," Aislinn said, feeling bad that she had pushed Baird away when she had needed him.

"Next time," Baird said simply and put her down. He turned to look for her luggage.

"That's it?"

A hanging dress bag and one small duffle sat on the bed.

Aislinn shrugged. "Well, it's only a weekend, isn't it?"

"I'm surprised. Typically girls have five more bags, one just for shoes and makeup."

"I've an editorial eye," Aislinn said stiffly and Baird laughed at her.

"It's not a bad trait to have, Ash."

She smiled at him as he picked up her bags.

"Think they've talked long enough to get over the awkwardness?"

"I certainly hope so as he is riding with her in the van to Dublin." Baird grinned widely at her as Aislinn gasped. She wagged her finger in front of his face.

"You're naughty."

"Me?" Baird raised his eyebrows mischievously and they laughed on their way down the stairs. A rush of adrenalin hit Aislinn and suddenly she felt energized and ready to take on the task. Stepping into the courtyard, she found Patrick instructing Morgan on the best way to load the paintings in her big conversion van.

"I want the last three, the biggest ones, on top," Aislinn called.

Patrick turned and nodded. "Aye, I figured they were special ones of sorts. We'll get it taken care of."

And take care of it they did. In under an hour they had the van packed and her little store looked barren. Aislinn looked around briefly before blowing a forlorn kiss to the empty walls. "I'll put something lovely up after I'm back, promise," she whispered to her shop and headed out to the courtyard, locking the door behind her.

Baird's neat sedan was parked in front of Morgan's gray conversion van. The three stood talking easily as Aislinn approached.

"All set?" Baird asked.

"Aye." Aislinn nodded and moved towards his sedan.

"See you two in Dublin," Baird called over his shoulder.

Aislinn bit her lip and tried not to laugh at Morgan's stricken expression.

"You're coming?" Morgan asked Patrick.

"Aye, want me to drive the first leg?" he asked easily.

"No, I've got it," Morgan said stiffly and hopped in the front seat of the van. Patrick turned and gave Aislinn and Baird the thumbs up and they both laughed at him before he swung into the passenger seat of the van, a huge grin on his face.

"Whoo, boy, wouldn't I pay to be in that van right now," Aislinn laughed as she buckled herself into the car. Reaching over to run her hand down Baird's arm, she smiled at him.

"Thank you for coming with me. It means a lot," she said.

"Wouldn't miss it for the world." Baird smiled down at

her and a warm glow filled her body and soothed the nerves that ate at her stomach.

HOURS LATER, Aislinn couldn't believe how quickly time had flown for her. Baird managed the curvy roads of the countryside with ease and conversation had never once waned for them. They laughed, argued, and challenged each other over pretty much every topic. Aislinn had never had so much fun on a road trip before.

The landscape coming out of Grace's Cove had been dreamy, but as they drew closer to Dublin, they stayed on the main thoroughfare and cars whipped past them as more city life began to crop up amongst the green landscape common to Ireland.

"What's the plan for when we get there?" Baird asked.

"We'll take the paintings straight to the gallery so they can unload and set up the show to their liking. We'll have almost the full day free tomorrow."

"And what do you have planned for that?"

Aislinn shrugged her shoulders and bit her lip, looking at the buildings streaming past her window.

"I don't know. Probably pace myself into a ball of nerves."

"Want to see where I went to school? I have to stop and pick up a manuscript from a colleague anyways. I've promised to edit a study he wants to publish."

"Sure, that would be nice. We can walk around the city and I'll play tourist while you show me your favorite college haunts." Aislinn smiled at him and tried to keep her mind from her show.

"You know, Green on Red Gallery is quite famous," Baird said smoothly, glancing over at her.

Aislinn only nodded in response, her mouth having suddenly gone dry.

"I can brag about my famous girlfriend now," Baird laughed. "As long as it doesn't start going to your head."

Aislinn mock punched him in the arm, her grin stretching her face wide. She felt like she could burst from happiness and nerves, all the emotions cluttering around inside her stomach.

"I wonder how Morgan and Patrick are doing." Aislinn twisted to see that the van was right behind them. She could see Patrick talking animatedly but couldn't make out much from Morgan.

"They'll be fine. They'll find their way…one way or the other," Baird said.

Aislinn settled back in her seat as they neared Dublin.

"Are we in the same hotel?" Aislinn asked, realizing that she had completely forgotten to book accommodations for Baird.

Baird only smiled at her.

"I've booked us a room at the Westbury."

"Oh, sounds lovely. Is it?"

Baird laughed. "Yes, the perfect hotel for an up-and-coming hot new artist."

"I'll have to call and cancel my room then. Oh, and ring the girls to see where they are staying."

"I've got them all in the same hotel," Baird said.

Aislinn whipped her head around to look at him in surprise.

"You're paying for all of them?"

Baird laughed. "Like their men would let me pay. No. But I am paying for Morgan, Patrick, and Fiona's rooms. As is my pleasure."

"Gosh, Baird. Thank you!"

"Of course." Baird smiled and then focused as the streets became more crowded. "I've got to slow down a bit to make sure that I don't lose Morgan on these city streets."

Aislinn quieted down and watched the buildings of Dublin pass by her window. She loved coming to the city but would never want to live there. Give her the ocean and small-town shops any day. She smiled at the mix of old and new that populated Dublin. Ancient churches crowded next to banks and pubs, each jostling for a position amongst the crowds that flowed through the streets. Baird flowed into the city center and allowed the traffic to funnel him around Trinity College towards the gallery.

"Do you know where the gallery is?"

"Aye, it's near a pub that I used to frequent," Baird said. He turned down a narrow back street and began to slow the car. "I'm pulling up in back as I assume that's where they will want you to unload."

Aislinn could only nod as he pulled to a stop behind a building that looked like a large warehouse with huge windows that ran the length of the building, allowing the natural light to seep into the rooms within. Her heart fluttered in her chest and Aislinn found that for a moment, she struggled to breathe.

"Shh, your work is magnificent. You'll be the talk of the town," Baird assured her and climbed out of the car. She watched him walk to the man standing by the back door and dug her clammy hands into her jeans.

"Okay. You've got this. And if nobody likes it...so what? You've got a fine business back home that you can barely keep up with," Aislinn said to herself and then pushed the door open to go meet with the man standing with Baird.

The man he spoke to turned and beamed at Aislinn. Tall, rail thin, and wearing a tweed smoking jacket with an honest-to-God monocle perched on his eye, he was fascinating and eccentric all in one package.

"You must be Aislinn. I'm Martin O'Hennesey, the art director."

"Martin, lovely to meet you in person finally," Aislinn said, grinning up at him, grateful that he wasn't some stiff and reserved art snob.

"We're ready to receive your work. Would you like to stay for a bit and help us to set up the show?"

Aislinn almost said no and then thought about how well Morgan had arranged her shop. She gestured to the van. "Can my assistant work with us? She's a great eye."

"Of course," Martin said smoothly and then turned to call into the building, where several men emerged to help. Aislinn turned to Baird.

"We may be a while."

"No problem, I'll steal Patrick for a pint," Baird assured. He leaned over and brushed a kiss over her lips, lingering for just a moment as the city sounds swirled around them.

"I'll call you later," Aislinn said, holding up her cell phone clutched in her hand.

"Do you need anything else from the car?"

"Just my pocket book."

Baird retrieved it while she went to talk to Morgan. Without any shame at all, Aislinn reached out and scanned Morgan and Patrick with her mind. She didn't even care when Morgan glared at her and gave her a mental shove back. Instead, she grinned widely at the girl, hooking her arm through Morgan's. She was happy to read that they seemed to have come to an uneasy truce. She wondered when they would admit their attraction for each other. Shrugging it off, she pointed a finger at Patrick.

"You, go with Baird. You'll receive a pint or two in reward for your service," Aislinn ordered. Patrick grinned at her and waved to them both as he ran to Baird's idling car.

"So?" Aislinn demanded.

"So, what? Where are they going?" Morgan said, stepping neatly around Aislinn's question.

"They are going to the pub. You and I are going to help set up the show."

Morgan squealed and bounced on her heels. "Really? I get to help?"

"I insisted."

Aislinn's breath whooshed out of her as Morgan flung her arms around Aislinn.

"Thank you, thank you, thank you!"

Aislinn untangled herself from Morgan and patted the girl on her arm. "You've got a good eye. You're an asset to my shop. Now, what do you think about setting it up by moods?"

"Let's take a look at the space and see," Morgan said, all business.

Turning, they walked into the gallery.

CHAPTER 36

*H*OURS LATER, AISLINN was ready for a pint herself.

Morgan had proved to be an invaluable asset and she and Martin had soon taken over the set-up of the pieces. They'd decided to flow the moods of the ocean through the various rooms until they reached the crowning glory.

Her three panels.

She stood back from them now as one of Martin's assistants adjusted the lighting to better highlight the paintings. A part of her stood in awe of her work. The panels covered the entire length of a wall and were stunning, demanding a response from the viewer. No person who looked at these paintings would remain unmoved.

Her eyes fell to the smallest bit of personal imagery that she added to the middle frame. The images were of her and Baird, walking the beach, their heads turned to look at the water as the faintest of glows pulsed from beneath the waves. Those who knew little of the cove would assume that it was just the sun hitting the waves in an odd way.

Fiona would know. As would the other girls.

She wondered what Baird would think when he saw it. If he would be angry with her for reminding him of a moment that both scared and perplexed him. Or if he would finally see the answer that he needed in her painting.

True love, Aislinn mused. The cove only glowed in the presence of true love. She'd known it to happen for others and had often wondered if it would happen for her. When it had, the force and sheer beauty of it had all but taken her under. She wished that Baird had reacted differently. That they could have stayed to watch the play of otherworldly light dance through the waters.

She'd been annoyed herself, Aislinn reminded herself. It hadn't just been Baird that had wanted to go.

I wasn't ready to see it, Aislinn whispered silently to the painting and traced her hand over their miniscule forms on the beach.

A gasp sounded behind her and then a long, slow clapping of hands. Aislinn tensed and turned to find Morgan with her hand covering her mouth and Martin smiling at her, applauding her with his long, thin hands.

"Bravo, my dear, bravo. Simply marvelous. I'm glad that you made us wait to see this piece," Martin said as he paced back and forth in front of her paintings, a look of pure bliss on his face.

"What will you call it?"

"The Revelation," Aislinn whispered.

"Yes, I love it. People will be lining up to purchase

this. We have some heavy hitters coming tomorrow and I suspect that this will be sold by the time the show is over."

Aislinn tried not to feel a bit weepy at the prospect of her paintings going to someone else. A part of her wanted to say that they weren't for sale.

"What…what if I don't want to sell them?"

Martin turned and scanned her face for a moment. Whatever he saw there made him nod slightly. "We'll take inquiries but not list it for sale. That way you can decide after the show and we'll let people know the price at that point. It makes it even more exclusive that way," Martin said.

Aislinn breathed a sigh of relief and beamed at the director. "Thank you."

"No problem. You've done a wonderful job with your show. I suspect it will be a huge success."

"What time do you need me tomorrow?"

"Hmm, I'd say around 6:00? That way you can go over any final changes you'd like made."

"I doubt there will be any. You've done a wonderful job with showcasing my work. Thank you," Aislinn said, reaching out her hand to shake Martin's.

"Ready to go, Morgan?"

The girl finally turned from the paintings, a sheen of tears in her eyes.

"I'm honored to know you," she whispered to Aislinn before wiping the tears from her eyes. Aislinn slung an arm over the girl's shoulders.

"No tears, come now."

"That's the best kind of art…the paintings that bring a

visceral reaction," Martin murmured and smiled at the women as he led them to the back door.

"I'm in need of a pint," Aislinn decided as she pulled out her phone and texted Baird.

"I think the hotel is fairly close," Morgan said and walked to her van. Aislinn followed and hopped into the front seat.

"Aye, looks like that's where they are at," Aislinn said, reading her text.

The night passed in a blur of laughter and good food. Aislinn had to keep pinching herself to believe that her friends were all here to celebrate her first art show.

She turned to look at Baird as he signed for the tab at the end of the night. His eyes smiled at her and a part of her just clicked into place. Knowing it was right.

It seemed like tomorrow would be the beginning of a whole new chapter in her life.

CHAPTER 37

SHE WAS RIGHT.

Having Baird with her definitely calmed her nerves. She'd even slept a little. Probably from sheer exhaustion, she thought as her lips quirked a smile back at her in the mirror. Baird was a particularly generous lover and he'd kept her up much of the night showcasing all of his fine abilities. Aislinn clipped her curls back from her face, knowing that the girls would style it for her later.

"Almost ready?"

Baird was taking her for a quick lunch and then to see his colleague at the university. In deference to walking around the city, she'd slipped on some tennis shoes, jeans, and a breezy tank top in a bright blue. Aislinn snagged a tote bag and a bright fuchsia scarf to wrap around her neck and met Baird at the door.

"All set." She beamed up at Baird and he bent to give her a quick kiss.

Aislinn felt like a schoolgirl, she thought later on, as Baird dragged her around his old stomping grounds. She'd stopped in pubs, gone to stores, and even walked through the park where he claimed that he had made the decision to become a psychiatrist. Aislinn didn't mind being dragged all over town as it was a beautiful day and it kept her from thinking too deeply about her show that evening. She'd done everything she could to make it a success. It was time to let go and let it ride.

"Ready to go meet Matthew?" Baird asked, smiling down at her as he slipped his hand through hers. They were walking through the main courtyard of Trinity College and Aislinn was admiring the architecture of the building.

"Sure, is he a psychiatrist too?"

"He is but he's moved more towards studying the brain…as in running experiments, studies, things of that sort. He likes to test his hypotheses and get results where I tend to like to work with people and see results that way."

"Both valid, in their own right," Aislinn said as he held open a door for her and they stepped into a long, cool corridor. A sleek black desk with a young woman on a computer was positioned in front of the hallway and Aislinn assumed it was a check-in of sorts.

The woman smiled brightly up at them. "Can I help you?"

"We are here to see Matthew. You can tell him it's Dr. Delaney," Baird said. The woman scanned her list and waved them on with her hand.

"You're all cleared. Head on back; he should be in his office or the lab."

Baird snagged Aislinn's hand again and they walked

along the corridor, passing doors with small desks piled with books, and people on the phone or grading papers.

Baird stopped her at an office door that had a small name sign reading: Matthew Connor, Ph.D. He poked his head in the door and then back out to smile at her.

"Must be in the lab."

They followed the corridor along to where the hall ended at a line of glass windows and a door. Through the window, Aislinn could see three men huddled over a table, looking through a pile of papers. Baird knocked lightly on the window and the men looked up. The man in the middle, who looked like a miniature version of Santa Claus, beamed at Baird and rushed over to open the door.

"Come in, come in," the man, who Aislinn presumed was Dr. Connor, boomed out, his voice matching her initial Santa Claus impression. He grabbed Baird in a fierce hug and then turned to peer at her.

"And this beautiful young lady?" he asked, grabbing her hand and pulling her further into the room. Aislinn found herself utterly charmed by him and laughed up at him as he led her towards the other men.

"This is Aislinn, a soon-to-be-famous artist, and my girlfriend," Baird said proudly, wrapping his arm around Aislinn's waist. She laughed lightly up at him and turned to the men.

"Pleased to meet you. Not quite famous, but an artist nonetheless," she said.

Dr. Connor's eyes narrowed and then a huge smile broadened across his face. Turning to the men next to him, he gestured at Aislinn.

"Gentlemen! This is the Aislinn that I was telling you

about. The one that Baird told us about. You know, with the extra-sensory abilities. I'm so happy he brought her to us."

An icy dredge of panic flicked through Aislinn's stomach and she separated herself from Baird, struggling to pull breath through a throat that was suddenly closing up.

"Oh yes, how wonderful. I'm so happy that you've agreed to let us study you," one of the other men beamed at her, pulling a notepad from a folder and slipping his glasses on. Dr. Connor, oblivious to the change in Aislinn, continued.

"Yes, when Baird first emailed me about you, I was so excited to make contact with someone who openly uses her extra abilities. We've been dying to get someone willingly in the lab so we can study the neural pathways that are used when you tune in to that side of yourself. We're hoping that we'll finally have an answer to why the brain sees what it does and can put a rest to this magick nonsense." Dr. Connor sniffed and then, finally focusing in on Baird and Aislinn, he stopped talking.

"What. Are. You. Talking. About?" Aislinn hissed through her teeth, her hand clenched to her stomach. Her whole body had seized up as though she had one huge muscle cramp and she forced herself to breathe shallowly as her mind tried to compartmentalize her emotions in order for her to focus on the words coming from Dr. Connor's mouth.

"Your ability? To study you?" Dr. Connor began and Baird cut him off.

"Didn't you receive my email? The one where I said

that I've started dating Aislinn and was no longer interested in pursuing that study?" Baird asked icily, turning to
move closer to Aislinn. She backed up, bumping into a
chair, her body trembling in shock.

In betrayal.

Dr. Connor shook his head in bewilderment. "No, I've
been in the lab most of this week. I'm sure that I'm fright-
fully behind on email. Is this…not what you wanted?"

"No, we don't want this," Baird said firmly and Aislinn
was startled to hear laughter cut through the room. She
froze when she realized it was coming from her.

"Is that what I am to you? A rat to be studied? So you
can satisfy your curiosity?" Aislinn asked Dr. Connor,
ripping her arm away from Baird's hand when he reached
for her.

"No, no, of course not, dear," Dr. Connor said and then
closed his mouth, finally realizing it was in his best
interest to shut up.

Aislinn turned to look at Baird, her entire body shaking
with betrayal. Nausea swirled in her stomach and her
world shifted beneath her, cracking. And in doing so, her
heart trembled and fell into the crevice that Baird had just
opened beneath her feet.

"You just couldn't let it go? Could you?" Hurt oozed
from her voice but she raised her hand to stop Baird's
approach. "You always have to have answers. To the point
that you were willing to submit me to this? To be some
sort of thing to be studied?"

Baird shook his head, not touching her. "No, nothing
like that. I promise, it was nothing like that."

"You want me to perform for them? Is that it? Fine,"

Aislinn said, rage overtaking the hurt that made it next to impossible for her to breathe. "This one on the left? He's tense right now, but fascinated by me nonetheless. And, he's wondering how much he can pay me to subject myself to a study. Nothing, by the way," Aislinn said. Turning, she looked over at Dr. Connor.

"Aislinn, stop. You have to listen."

"Dr. Connor is also fascinated by me but he seems to have a bit more of a heart because he is also having trouble watching this as it's painful for him. He doesn't like to see people hurt." Aislinn bowed her head to Dr. Connor, silently thanking him.

"And this one?" Aislinn pointed at the last man in the room. "He thinks this is funny. So I've a mind to tell you what you can go and do." She jerked her hands at him, pretending to do magick, and the man flinched and yelped.

Aislinn turned, finally meeting Baird's eyes.

"And you. I don't care what you're feeling. You took my private world and spewed it in front of them for their excitement and perusal. I allowed myself to be vulnerable to you." Aislinn shook her head at him, forcing tears back from her eyes, promising herself a long vacation in Greece if she could hold the tears back. She wouldn't give Baird that.

She'd already given him enough.

Aislinn tore from the room, racing down the corridor.

"Aislinn!" Baird shouted after her, his feet pounding on the hard linoleum floor. Aislinn saw the woman at the front desk talking to a man that looked like security. They both turned at the shout.

"Security!" Aislinn screamed and the man ran to her.

"This man. Stop him. I must get away safely," Aislinn shouted at him as she continued running. She heard Baird curse as the security guard intercepted him but Aislinn refused to look back.

Leaving her heart in the science building, she ran for the hotel, gasping and trying not to cry. Aislinn tore into the lobby in a panic and pressed the button to the elevator, praying that it would come quickly.

"Aislinn!"

Aislinn refused to look up, afraid that she would break down in the lobby where several people milled about, waiting for others.

The door opened and Aislinn ran into the elevator, grateful that the car was empty.

"Aislinn!" Cait whipped through the doors just as they closed behind her. She stared in awe at Aislinn and reached out to grab her arm.

"Oh no. Oh, honey, what happened?"

Aislinn just shook her head, terrified that if she spoke, everything would come flooding out and she would never pull herself together for her show. Cait narrowed her eyes at Aislinn as she read her mind.

"That bastard! I'll skin him myself." Cait swore up a storm, her pub owner's roots showing through. Aislinn almost cracked a smile at her violent outburst. Almost.

"Okay, okay, just breathe. Let's go to your room and get your stuff. You'll come with me?"

Aislinn nodded. She was grateful when Cait didn't ask anything else, just simply reached out and held her hand. There were times when talking was just too hard.

The elevator doors dinged, and Aislinn ran to her

room, fumbling in her pocketbook for her key card. She slipped it in the lock and rushed to where she had packed most of her stuff in the morning in anticipation of going to the girls' rooms to get ready for the show. Grateful that there was little to gather, she stopped by the pad of paper by the bed. Bending over, her arms full of stuff, she scrawled a message across the paper and then ripped it off, tossing it on the bed.

Stay away from me.

Cait nodded her approval and rushed her from the room, turning her down the hallway towards the staircase.

"We're only a floor below you. Let's skip the elevator in case he comes up."

Aislinn nodded at Cait and together, their arms full of clothes and shoes and luggage, they clattered down the stairs to Cait's floor.

"We've an adjoining suite with Keelin. Go in. I'll ring her and fill her in," Cait said as she unlocked the door and swept the door open so Aislinn could race past her. Aislinn stumbled into the room and dropped her stuff across the large bed and then turning, desperately looked for the bathroom. Spying the door, she ran in, dropped to her knees and proceeded to throw up her pain.

Aislinn heard voices in the room, but couldn't bring herself to look up from the toilet. She flushed and then sat back on her knees, waiting to see if her stomach had settled.

"Here, honey, let me." Keelin walked into the room and knelt beside her. She put her hands on Aislinn's stomach and closed her eyes. Aislinn felt a ripple of energy wash through her and in a second, her nausea was gone. She turned to Keelin with grateful eyes.

"Can you heal a broken heart?" Aislinn whispered.

Keelin shook her head and wrapped her arms around Aislinn.

"I would if I could, sweetie, I really would. Come on, let's get you some water."

Keelin pulled Aislinn up from the cool tile floor and Aislinn followed her into the room. A door from the bedroom led to a connecting living room. Shane and Flynn hovered over Cait, their faces clouded in anger.

"Oh no," Aislinn whispered.

"It's fine. They'll only break a few bones, promise," Keelin said lightly and then laughed at Aislinn's face. The men looked up at their voices and Cait turned.

"We'll kill him," Shane said simply and Cait reached out and swatted him.

"Sure and I don't need a murderer for this baby's father, now, do I?" she asked him.

"No, thank you. Please, do nothing. If you do something then it means it is important to me. And…he's nothing," Aislinn said softly.

"Ash," Keelin began, running her hand down Aislinn's arm.

"Nothing. It's nothing. I'm a big girl and I will get over this. Now, I need you ladies to work extra hard on making me look amazing tonight." She stopped and turned as she walked towards her pile of clothes. "Oh, and don't hurt Baird. But, I don't want him at my show. Understood?"

"We'll take care of it," Flynn said evenly and Aislinn nodded.

"I don't want to talk about it. I don't want to give it more power than it already has. I have to focus on tonight. Please, distract me," Aislinn begged as she sat in a chair, and Keelin brought her bag of makeup over.

"Flynn is looking at buying another restaurant along the river here," Keelin said and Aislinn smiled at her, grateful for the bond that she and her half-sister had built through the year, and for her tight-knit support group.

She couldn't have imagined what would have happened if they hadn't been here.

"Fantastic, I'll paint something for the walls," Aislinn said and smiled up at Keelin. "Now, make me beautiful."

CHAPTER 38

*S*HE WAS GONE.

After Baird had sorted things out with the security guard and convinced him that he wasn't out to hurt Aislinn, he had run to the door to see that the courtyard was empty. As he'd made to leave, Matthew had stopped him.

"Baird, I'm so sorry, I thought that was why you had brought her with you. It was an honest mistake," Matthew had panted at his side, his cheeks pink with embarrassment.

And, it had been. An honest mistake.

Because at the beginning, before he really knew where things were going with Aislinn, he had emailed Matthew with questions. It was part of his nature to question things that he didn't understand and to seek answers. When Matthew had invited Baird to bring Aislinn up to see if she would like to try to learn more about how her ability worked, Baird had left it open-ended.

We'll see, he'd written. Baird shook his head as he thought about those words.

He'd fallen for Aislinn soon after that email.

When Baird had known that he was coming to Dublin with her, he had emailed Matthew and explained that their relationship had changed and that he didn't want or need answers about Aislinn anymore. And, that he suspected that she wouldn't take kindly to Matthew's inquiries about it. It appeared that Matthew had never gotten his email.

Baird crumpled her note between his hand, fury and sadness raging through him at her words. Stay away from her. Like he was some kind of hooligan that would hurt her.

Except he had hurt her.

His own disbelief and refusal to accept what she was had done this to her. Baird never should have tried to research it, not after they'd slept together. He'd violated her trust – right from the start. He laughed derisively at himself. God, even when he'd told her that he loved her he had condescended to her about her gift. When had he turned into such a high-minded jerk? He'd held a beautiful, astonishingly creative, and exceptionally sensitive woman in his arms and through his own blindness, he'd let her slip away.

He didn't even know if he could fight for her.

"You could go to the show, you know." A voice, rich like a warm brandy, paralyzed him for a moment. Goose-bumps stood out on his arms and the room felt like it had been plunged into an ice locker. Slowly, he turned.

A woman sat in the chair by the window, resplendent in a red velvet dress, her hair pulled back in intricate knots with a silver chain woven through it. Her eyes dominated in a face that was both beautiful and intimidating. Strength radiated from her, as did an otherworldly aura. Baird's mouth went dry.

"I'm sorry, but have we met? Did Aislinn tell you to come here?" Baird tilted his head at the strange woman, confused by her presence, not sure why she made him want to reach for a weapon. Something was off about her.

A smile flitted across the woman's beautiful face. "No, Aislinn did no such thing. I presume then that you don't know who I am?" She tilted her head and waited for Baird to speak.

Baird could feel his heart beating, as though someone was playing a drum against his chest, and his fingers tightened involuntarily until he dug his nails into his palms.

"No," Baird whispered.

She stood and Baird stumbled back, his legs hitting the bed, his butt following shortly thereafter. When she'd stood and moved away from the chair...he could see the chair through her. Baird gulped and shot his eyes towards the door. Could he run for it?

"Oh stop it. I mean you no harm. I'm Grace O'Malley, and Aislinn is descended of my blood. You should consider yourself honored that I've chosen to show myself to you. Rarely do I make my presence known except for those lucky enough to share my blood." Grace raised her chin and looked down at him, every inch the pirate queen that great lore made her out to be.

Baird tried to regulate his breathing. Was he dreaming? Hallucinating?

"Stop questioning how this is. I've little time here, now

pay attention," Grace barked at him and Baird jerked to attention, nodding at her as she began to pace. His stomach swam a bit as he could see the pictures on the wall through her shadowy form.

"You've insulted Aislinn, and everyone of my blood for that matter," Grace began. Baird opened up his mouth to speak but Grace held up her hand to stop his words.

"That being said, I understand that men can be foolish and should be given second chances."

Baird wanted to speak but wisely kept his mouth shut. There was little sense in arguing with a ghost.

"You must go to her. She doesn't trust you right now. Go to her, find the revelation. You'll know what to do then," Grace said.

"The revelation?" Baird asked in confusion.

"Go to her. You've hurt her. Prove your love," Grace ordered and as Baird opened his mouth to speak, she faded from the room. Baird jumped up and ran to where she had stood. Putting his hands on his hips, he scanned the room, looking for any video cameras or projection monitors that would have been able to fake this apparition.

And, God help him, he let out a shriek when he was shoved by something that he couldn't see.

"Okay, okay, I'm sorry. Yes, I see that you are real," Baird shouted into the empty room. Message received, he thought. Stop questioning what you don't know. Sinking down onto the bed, Baird ran Aislinn's note through his hands again. He glanced at his watch to see that the show would be starting in an hour. Baird suspected that Aislinn was still in the hotel, probably getting ready in one of the girls' rooms. And, in all likelihood, the men would be out to harm him.

As though on cue, there was a knock at the door. Baird sighed, anticipating what was coming. Peeking through the peephole in the door, he quickly debated not answering.

"We can see you," Flynn called through the door.

Baird sighed and opened the door, holding his palms up immediately.

"I'm in love with her," he said and closed his eyes as Shane's fist stopped mere inches from his face.

"Great control, lad," Flynn said and patted Shane on the shoulder. Baird stepped back and motioned for the men to come in. Shane and Flynn sat on the bed while Patrick paced, an unhappy look on his face.

"You've gone and made a mess of things," Flynn began.

"Aye, I know. I truly didn't mean to hurt her, but she gave me little time to explain before she ran off," Baird said.

"Explain now," Patrick demanded and Baird turned, raising an eyebrow at the young man.

"Aye, he's a feisty one. I can attest to that," Shane said.

Baird ran through a brief explanation and then said, "Listen, it's in my nature to question things. It isn't even out of judgment. I just like to seek answers. I'm trained in trying to figure things out. It never came from a place of wanting to hurt her."

Flynn chuckled and Shane shot him a nasty look.

"Well, I'm just laughing at the fact that he tried to

figure out a woman. One of ours, at that. I mean, hasn't he learned that one can never really understand women?"

Baird cracked a smile at that, though his heart still raced in his chest from his encounter with Grace.

"How do you, uh, deal with that? With your women having power?" Baird asked and then cast his eyes to Flynn. "Wait, does Keelin have power?"

"Aye, she can heal with her hands," Flynn said matter of factly and then chuckled when Baird's mouth dropped open in shock. "Suspend disbelief, my dear boy. Some-times there are no explanations."

Baird shook his head, reeling at the idea that pretty Keelin was able to heal someone with her hands. He turned and raised an eyebrow at Shane.

"Yes, Cait can read minds. She turns it off for the most part or is really good at hiding it. It's a gift as much as a curse to her. It isn't easy always being able to hear people's thoughts shooting through your head," Shane said. Baird hadn't thought about it like that. He supposed that it had to be hard for Aislinn to always be exposed to people's feel-ings, never having a filter of sorts.

Which made him feel even worse as he began to realize that her ability was both a gift and a curse.

"I'm an idiot," Baird finally sighed and threw up his hands.

"Fix it," Flynn ordered and turned a steely look on Baird. "And, if you don't, I'll see you run out of Grace's Cove. I don't need violence like this one." Flynn gestured to where Shane sat, a wicked grin on his face.

"She doesn't want me to go to the show tonight."

"Aye, we've been instructed to keep you away," Flynn said.

The men sat in silence as they surveyed each other for a moment.

"We could agree to not see him?" Patrick spoke up.

"I'm okay with that on one condition," Flynn said, raising his hand. "If, even for a moment, she looks unhappy, you're out. Got it? This is her night and nothing, I mean nothing at all, is to stop her from having a good night. So figure out a way to make it happen or don't come at all."

Baird nodded at him. "I have no idea how to do that, but I will think of something."

The men nodded, casting pitying looks on Baird as they filed from his room. Baird stayed where he was, his hand closed around her note, as his mind whirled.

Fiona.

CHAPTER 39

"**O**PEN UP, I can see you." Baird echoed the words that Flynn had just said at his door mere moments ago.

Fiona cracked the door and sniffed at him. "And, why should I let you in?"

"I just saw Grace O'Malley."

Fiona's eyes widened and without a word, she opened the door and motioned for Baird to enter her room.

"Whiskey?" Fiona asked, and Baird looked at her in surprise. A bottle of Redbreast 12 sat on the sideboard in her room.

"Please."

Resplendent in a woolen navy dress with silver thread-ing, her hair tied back in an intricate knot, and sparkly drops at her ears, Fiona looked every inch the descendent of his ghostly visitor. Fiona plucked an ice cube from the ice bucket and dropped it in a glass, before pouring a generous splash of the whiskey in the glass. She moved to Baird and offered him the glass.

"Slàinte," she said and clinked her glass to his. "Speak."

"Have you heard what happened with Aislinn?"

"Of course," Fiona said, not pretending to play coy. Baird appreciated her directness.

"I love her. It's a huge misunderstanding," Baird said. Fiona only nodded, piercing him with her steely gaze as she took a sip from her glass.

"That's some misunderstanding. I suppose there is a lesson in it for you though," Fiona murmured and Baird cracked a smile at her.

"Aye, as I'm seeing now," he said.

"Why do you think that it was Grace O'Malley that you saw?" Fiona asked.

"Why did she appear to me? She said that she didn't show herself to those not of her blood," Baird said.

Fiona raised an eyebrow at him. "So, it was her."

"That I know of. But, seeing you dressed up and having just seen her, I can see the resemblance. You're both powerful beauties," Baird said.

Fiona beamed at him and crossed the room to gather her purse and a wrap.

"Thank you, I appreciate the compliment. Especially at my age. Now, I must be leaving shortly. Tell me what Grace said."

"She told me to go to the show. To find the revelation. That I would have my answer then." Baird bit his lip, wondering how he would do this without upsetting Aislinn further. He looked up at Fiona. "I need your help."

Fiona was silent for a moment as she thought about it.

"Let me call Flynn. I'm supposed to ride with them. Do they know?"

"Yes," Baird said.

Fiona pulled a sleek cell phone from her pocket and rang Flynn. After a few murmured words, she flipped it closed and put it back in her purse.

"It looks like you're my date. Shall we?"

Baird breathed out a sigh of relief. Then he looked at Fiona, worry filling his mind.

"She never said she loved me, you know. I just realized that. Maybe I shouldn't do this. Maybe she doesn't love me."

Fiona tilted her head, considering his words.

"What do you feel?"

"I guess I felt like she did, which is probably why I didn't realize until now that she had never said it back to me," Baird said, lifting his shoulders in a defeated shrug.

"So, tonight you have to fight for an unknown result then," Fiona clarified.

"I...I guess that I do."

Fiona chuckled and Baird narrowed his eyes at her.

"I just love how life continues to teach us lessons. Now, is that what you are wearing?"

"No, I must change quickly if you don't mind waiting."

"Please do. I'll finish my whiskey and consider your approach."

CHAPTER 40

*A*ISLINN RAN HER sweaty palms over her purse, nervously chewing at her lip. Her entire body hurt and all she wanted to do was crawl into bed with a pint of ice cream and a fluffy romance novel.

Romance, she snorted to herself. Right. Like that would help her frame of mind.

"Everything will be just fine," Cait murmured from behind her and Keelin whipped her head around.

"What? Is she thinking about Baird again?" Keelin asked.

"I'm right here," Aislinn said, raising her hand.

They were in the car on the way to the show, sandwiched together in the rows of Flynn's sleek SUV.

"You look fantastic. Have we mentioned how great you look? All because of us, of course. I think that we should be stylists, don't you, Cait?" Keelin asked sweetly and Cait rolled her eyes at Keelin. Aislinn knew that she was trying to distract her and was grateful for it.

"The red was a good choice," Cait agreed.

At the last moment, Aislinn had slipped from the purple beaded column dress to the red dress that made her look like she was on fire. To her, red signaled power. She didn't want to let Baird take her power from her.

"That necklace is fabulous," Keelin said, running her hands over the linked circles that had taken Aislinn more hours than she wanted to think about to create. It was a piece of art in itself and the dress showcased it perfectly.

"It's a one and only. I don't know if I have the patience to make another."

"If you do, let me know. I know about a million people back in Boston who would fall all over themselves for it," Keelin said.

Aislinn smiled at her and then gasped as Flynn turned the corner to the gallery. Keelin squealed and gripped her arm tightly. Aislinn grabbed her hand and held it, clenching tightly, forcing herself to breathe shallowly through her mouth as she gaped at the long line of people that stood waiting to walk the red carpet into the gallery.

"Is this for me?" Aislinn whispered.

"Aye, it says Red on Green Gallery outside," Shane said.

"Shane, stop it. She knows it is for her. She's having herself a moment," Cait said, narrowing her eyes at her fiancé.

Shane motioned zipping his mouth shut as Flynn slowed to a crawl behind a long line of cars.

"Do you want to walk the red carpet or go around back?"

Aislinn thought about it. What she really wanted to do was sneak in the back door. Which meant she needed to walk the red carpet. As an artist, she'd learned that when something made her uncomfortable, that meant that she needed to push through it. Taking the comfortable route never led to breakthroughs or personal growth. She took a deep breath.

"Red carpet," Aislinn said.

"I'll get out and run ahead, talk to security," Shane offered and slipped from the SUV. Aislinn watched him approach two men in suits and then gesture to the car. They nodded and waved towards the door. Aislinn saw Martin step from the front doors of the gallery and she smiled at his gray paisley suit. The man had a style all his own, she thought.

Martin waved their car forward and panic gripped Aislinn.

"What if I trip?"

"Then you get up, silly," Cait said easily and Aislinn stopped herself.

So what if she tripped? That was what life was all about. The moods of her paintings reflected that. The ocean whispered her secrets to anyone that wanted to listen. Pain, joy, love, anger, and sadness….all were a part of the human experience. The point wasn't to avoid the emotions. It was to embrace them and live life through them, as majestically and flamboyantly as the dramatic waters of the sea did.

A chill swept over Aislinn and for a moment, she felt like something soft brushed against her cheek. Instantly, a calm settled through her and she straightened her shoulders, shifting herself to turn so that she could easily step from the car.

"Ready?"

"I'm ready," Aislinn said and waited until the door opened before stepping into a blinding flash of light from the crowd of cameras that lined the red carpet. She'd never experienced anything like it before. Martin was immediately by her side, hooking his arm through hers, and she was grateful for his support. Cait snagged her purse from her and together, she and Martin posed for reporters and answered questions.

"You look magnificent, my dear. Like a flame that is devouring itself," Martin whispered to her and she turned to smile at him, grateful for his support.

"I'm sorry that I couldn't get here earlier," she whispered.

"No need, your show is flawless. One of the easiest that I've ever had to set up," Martin assured her and they swept through the slick doors of the gallery and Aislinn gasped.

"Oh...oh I'm going to cry," Aislinn whispered and Martin immediately pulled a handkerchief from his pocket.

"It was Morgan's idea."

"It was spot on. I need to give her a raise," Aislinn said. She had wondered where Morgan had disappeared to earlier today.

What looked like thousands of candles ran the length of the room, clustered on driftwood-style pillars and small tables. Clear glass votive holders lined pathways through the gallery while larger pillar-style candles were clustered in odd groupings on the tables. It was the only light in the gallery aside from the soft lights that highlighted the paintings and the effect turned the gallery into a mystical, enchanting underwater cave. Her paintings raged across the walls while the candles flickered softly, the movement of the light seeming to make the waters of her paintings roll and dance.

It was the most exciting and humbling thing that Aislinn had ever experienced.

"I can't believe that these are mine," Aislinn breathed.

Martin nodded in agreement. "Every great artist has a tendency to step back, as though emerging from a cloud, to look at what they've created and wonder...how did that come from me?"

Aislinn nodded at Martin. He understood.

"That doesn't mean you are a fraud, my dear. It just means that you are so immersed in your work that you don't always step back to see the bigger picture. And, this, oh this bigger picture, it's magnificent," Martin purred and pulled her through the line of candles as her paintings writhed in emotion around her, to her masterpiece.

The Revelation.

The panels were hung perfectly on the wall, and what had to be a thousand candles lined the floor in front of it, creating a barrier between people and the painting. The light danced across the panels and the painting was haunting, ethereal, and like a punch to her gut.

Aislinn looked at the glow from the cove and the softly lit figures that walked the sand beach. Turning, she looked at Martin.

"Sell it," she said flatly.

Martin drew back, his eyes wide in awe...and concern. "You're quite sure?"

"Yes," Aislinn said simply and turned to where a line of people stood at the doors. "Shall we get started?"

"Of course, let's get you set up over here with your friends to start." Martin motioned to where Cait and Keelin and the others stood in the corner. She saw Morgan peeking out from behind the group, clad in a black knit dress, looking like a model having just stepped off the Paris fashion runways.

"Morgan!" Aislinn exclaimed and ran to her, wrapping her arms around the girl and pulling her in. Morgan stiffened for just a moment and then allowed herself to be hugged by Aislinn. It was a big improvement from her earlier days of refusing to be touched, Aislinn noted and then drew back from the girl.

"Thank you, thank you, thank you. You've brought my show to life," Aislinn whispered.

"No, it was just an idea; your paintings needed a moody sort of lighting is all that I could think." Morgan shrugged it off but Aislinn grasped her arm and turned her to look out at the gallery.

"No, look at this. Really look at it. You've talent. We are going to talk more about this when we get back home. I think that I have some ideas on a direction for you…if you'd like?" Aislinn raised her eyebrow in question at Morgan and the girl nodded furiously.

"Aye, I'd love that."

Turning, she nodded at Martin and he pushed the doors open, inviting the waiting crowd of people.

"Ready? I'm going to say that I knew you when you weren't famous," Cait declared and snagged an appetizer from a passing waiter with a tray.

Aislinn laughed at her and turned to greet the incoming crowd of people.

AN HOUR LATER, Aislinn's head was dizzy. She'd had her cheek pinched, her shoulder patted, and more than one invitation to dinner. People had congratulated her, condescended to her, and asked to commission her work. Her head spun at the craziness of it all.

Stepping back from the latest art buyer, who was trying to discuss painting technique and her motivation for one of the fury paintings, she reached for a glass of champagne to cool her dry throat.

The crowd swirled around her and Aislinn could see more than one discreet SOLD sticker on the paintings that lined the walls. She couldn't bring herself to look at The Revelation.

A flash of red caught her eye and she turned to see Fiona sailing through the crowd, her arms full of red poppies.

For a moment, just a brief second, happiness filled her as she thought about Baird. She crushed the thought down, refusing to think about him, knowing that if she did, the cold knot in her stomach would seep through her until it overtook the joy from the experience of her first show.

Fiona stopped before her and smiled up at her.

"Flowers? For me?" Aislinn smiled, refusing to think about how closely they matched the bouquet that Baird had given her just a day ago.

"For you," Fiona said, and as Aislinn reached to take them, she glanced up and across the room.

For a moment, time stood still and she could have sworn that she saw Baird standing in front of The Revelation. Her heart stopped and, stricken, she raised her arm to say something, to motion to security to have him removed.

Fiona grabbed her arm and turned her, pulling her towards a quiet corner, Aislinn tried to look over her shoulder, but the old woman was speaking to her.

"There's a card," Fiona said, her words finally penetrating the fog that hung around Aislinn's head.

"Oh, what? Oh," Aislinn said and looked down at the glowing bouquet of flowers in her arms. The petals so closely matched the color of her dress, it was hard to see where one stopped and the other started. Dipping her hands into the blooms, she pulled a small card from the depths of the bouquet.

I believe in you. Can you believe in us?

Aislinn's heart clenched and tears threatened to fill her eyes. Fiona reached out and grabbed her arm, and as a small tingle of energy washed through her, Aislinn's eyes cleared.

"I don't usually do that, but there should only be tears of happiness tonight, my child," Fiona said and Aislinn raised her eyes, grateful for Fiona's help.

"He's here?" Aislinn breathed.

"He'll not disturb you. But the question on the card is valid," Fiona said.

"What? You're on his side?" Aislinn raised her eyebrows in shock at Fiona.

"I'm on the side of love," Fiona said easily, smiling up at her.

"He hurt me," Aislinn breathed.

"Aye, and it won't be the last time," Fiona said. "That's the thing with love…with emotions. It's messy. Things become intertwined, feelings hurt, and it's only true love when you seek to understand the other person's motivations and agree to forgive. That is the type of love that grows over the ages. A lasting, forgiving love."

"So you want me to forgive him?" Aislinn asked.

Fiona laughed and gestured around to the paintings that raged across the walls.

"You need to look to yourself for that answer, my dear. But, ask yourself this…why didn't you tell him that you loved him? What are you afraid of?"

Aislinn stopped, ready to defend herself, and then her eyes went to the trio of paintings across the room.

"I'm afraid that he won't love me or accept me…all of me," Aislinn whispered.

"And what happens if he doesn't?"

Aislinn shrugged her shoulders. "Then I pick myself up, paint through my heartbreak and move on."

"Exactly. The world won't stop for you. But what if he does…love you. All of you?"

Aislinn felt a warmth flow through her and she smiled at Fiona. "Then my world opens up, my life moves on, but with him by my side."

Fiona nodded at her.

"Exactly. Two different paths through this world. In both, you'll find your way through. One way might bring you more happiness, is all." Fiona reached up and kissed her cheek. "It seems to me that you have a decision to make."

"You're right. And, here I am, acting all hurt and heartbroken when I never even told him that I loved him. And he all but did everything he could to help make this show a success." Guilt churned at Aislinn suddenly.

Fiona turned a commanding gaze on Aislinn. "I'm not saying that the man doesn't deserve a little butt-kicking. I'm just saying that you have some thinking to do. Oh, and that I am so incredibly proud of you. Would you just look at this?" Fiona swept her arm out to the packed gallery, illuminated by candlelight and the emotions of her paintings. Aislinn caught a glimpse of her mother flirting with Martin and smiled. "It's beyond words. You, my dear, are a power to be reckoned with. Never have I seen such emotion simply bleed from paintings before. I've already purchased one and I'm considering another."

"Fiona! I would have given you one," Aislinn said, her mouth dropping open.

"Absolutely not! I can dine out on purchasing your work for years to come and I'll raise my nose in the air and crow about knowing a famous artist that shows in Dublin." Fiona's eyes twinkled up at her and Aislinn bent to crush the old woman to her chest, not caring if the flowers got damaged.

"You saved me, you know."

"Nonsense. You saved yourself. Now, think about what I've said. Choices to make," Fiona said and then pulled away to follow a waiter with a tray of champagne.

Aislinn looked down at the poppies in her arms.

Choices.

She spied Martin through the crowd and moved through people, holding her hand up politely as people rushed to talk to her. Finally reaching Martin, she pulled him aside.

"Those poppies are fantastic," Martin enthused, looking down at her flowers.

"Martin, don't sell The Revelation," Aislinn whispered to him.

A stricken look crossed the man's face.

"Darling, I'm sorry, I've just completed the paperwork."

"What? You sold it already?"

"Yes, there was a huge line of people that wanted it. I sold to the highest offer. Astronomical price. You'll make out quite handsomely." Martin smiled down at her and Aislinn pasted a polite smile on her face as her heart cracked.

Turning, she walked to her paintings and stood before them, ignoring the crowd of people that surged around her. Her heart hammered in her chest and she struggled to breathe as she realized what she was giving up.

And the realization that it was more than just her paintings.

CHAPTER 41

*L*ATE THAT NIGHT, Aislinn was still trying to wipe the silly grin off her face. The show had been a smashing success and every painting had sold.

Including The Revelation.

Aislinn shook her head as she forced herself to tamp down on the panic that raced through her at the thought of losing those paintings. With the proceeds from the sales, she planned to harass Martin until he gave her the name of the buyer and then she would buy them back.

Aislinn approached the night manager at the front desk. He smiled brightly at her as she tottered towards him on her heels, half-buzzed from the champagne she'd drunk at dinner after the show.

"Can I help you, miss?"

"Yes, can you tell me if the man in room 338 has checked out? Baird Delaney?"

"One moment, please."

The man scanned his computer and then smiled politely at her.

"Yes, it looks like he checked out around 6:00 pm today."

Before her show. It hadn't been Baird that she had seen at the show after all.

Aislinn tried to push away the sadness that covered her.

Nodding her thanks, she went to the elevators to head to Fiona's room. She had an extra bed in her suite and tomorrow, Aislinn had agreed to ride home with Fiona on the train. It would give her time to decompress from the show without having to talk to people for hours in the car. Fiona knew the power of silence for healing the heart and Aislinn had had her fill of people, of emotions, of absorbing the impact of having an extra gift in the crowds of people that wanted to interact with her. It was positively exhausting trying to keep her mental shields up.

THE NEXT MORNING, Aislinn found herself squished against the window of a train, idly watching the country-side zip by in a state of sheer exhaustion.

She was right, she thought. She did sleep better with Baird around. Aislinn allowed her eyes to unfocus a little so that the countryside blurred past her and she tried to convince her mind to nod off and sleep. Unfortunately, it wasn't working. She sighed and crossed her arms over her chest, continuing the refrain that had plagued her all night.

Why hadn't she told Baird that she loved him?

Not that he was off the hook for hurting her, but – and this was the downside to her gift – she also knew how he felt about her. Like, *really knew*. And, there had been no subterfuge in his behavior or any underlying motives the day that they had gone to his school. She would have been able to feel it a mile away.

So why did she let herself become enraged with him if she knew – truly knew – that he had meant her no harm?

It was still hurtful, what he had done, she reminded herself. Through the night, as she had tossed and turned, the real reason had finally worked its way to the foreground of her mind.

She was afraid of commitment.

Maybe because she came from a broken home. Or, perhaps it was because she viewed commitment as a responsibility and much of her life as an artist had been based on eschewing responsibilities and following her own path. And, she'd finally reached the conclusion that just because she was afraid of something didn't mean that she shouldn't try it. Typically when something frightened her, she challenged it or jumped in feet first. She couldn't be scared of being hurt, Aislinn lectured herself. Look at the beautiful paintings she had created in the midst of her fury. Could she really call herself an artist if she refused to allow herself to feel the full spectrum of human emotion, both good and bad?

Uncomfortable with the turn that her thoughts had taken and knowing that she most likely owed at least a small portion of an apology to Baird, Aislinn sighed again.

"Huffing and puffing isn't going to make this train move any faster," Fiona murmured and Aislinn shot her a grin.

"I'm glad that you came with me, thank you," Aislinn said.

"Of course. I can't wait to hang my paintings when they arrive."

"I could have had Morgan bring them back with her."

"Nonsense. And miss having the cute delivery man come to my cottage? Never."

Aislinn chuckled at Fiona, loving her presence and enjoying the soothing effect that Fiona inevitably had upon her. It was easy to lose herself in the rhythm of the train, the clicking of the wheels against the rails, the exhaustion that pressed against her eyes. She promised herself that she would take a sleeping pill when she got home, just simply fall face down in her bed and hide from the world. Just for a day.

"Ah, Fiona. What am I going to do?"

"Paint more paintings, become world famous, let Morgan run your shop." Fiona shrugged her shoulders.

"You know what I'm talking about," Aislinn said.

Fiona dipped her head and looked at Aislinn over her reading glasses. "Sure and you aren't thinking that I'm going to tell you what to do with your love life."

Aislinn looked back out of the window, the green landscape sliding past her, and grimaced.

"I think that I owe him an apology."

"So apologize," Fiona said simply.

"You make it sound so easy," Aislinn protested.

"It is. Nobody ever feels worse after giving an apology, you know," Fiona commented.

It was hard to argue with Fiona's wisdom. "But don't you think that he owes me an apology as well?"

"Yes, he does. You both do. So do it and be done with it. Why waste time being miserable?"

"Because that's what artists do, duh," Aislinn laughed at her.

She was right though, Aislinn thought as she settled back into silence. Why waste time being miserable indeed?

CHAPTER 42

HER SHOP LOOKED barren, its walls bereft of paintings. Aislinn closed the door behind her and went inside, tossing her bags on her desk before walking in a circle around the empty shop.

The room seemed to echo the emptiness she felt inside and she realized how much she had gotten used to hearing Baird's voice every day. It was like a light had extinguished in her soul.

With a shake of her head, she snagged her luggage from the desk and ran up the stairs to her bedroom. All Aislinn wanted to do was not think about anything for a moment and slip beneath her covers for a good solid nap.

"Oh, yeah, this is what I need," she murmured to herself as she stripped down to her tank and underwear and slid beneath the cool sheets. In a matter of moments, the exhaustion finally caught up with her and she slipped into sleep.

. . .

A POUNDING on the back door awoke her. She sat straight up and for a moment, couldn't remember where she was. The room was dark and as she whipped her head around, she remembered that she was in her own bed.

"Coming!" Aislinn shouted down and flipped on the light by her bed. She bent over the side of the bed and snagged her jeans. Grabbing a sweatshirt from a coat hook by her bed, she pulled it over her head and tossed her curls back, allowing them to tumble down her back.

Aislinn padded down the stairs and opened the door a crack, peeking out into her back courtyard.

Nobody was there.

"Hello?" Aislinn called and stepped onto her back stoop.

Her heart skidded and skipped a beat as she saw a single red poppy sitting on her picnic table. Aislinn's breath hitched and she stepped further into the courtyard.

"Baird?"

Silence greeted her words and that is when she saw the second poppy. This one lay on the ground, a few feet from the table. Confused, Aislinn walked closer and saw another poppy a few feet further from the second. Bending to pick up the first two, she moved closer to the third, bent to pick it up, raised her head and saw another at the open gate to her courtyard.

The gate was never left open, she thought, and scurried to close it, picking up another poppy on the way.

As her hand fell on the smooth wood of the gate, she saw another poppy a few feet out. Aislinn leaned over the gate and tilted her head to see a row of poppies lining the sidewalk and disappearing around the corner.

A laugh, bordering on slightly hysterical, broke from her lips and Aislinn raced down the sidewalk, bending to collect the flowers, following her heart as she raced down the flower trail that Baird had left for her. The flowers wound down the sidewalk in front of her store and as she brought her head up, she realized that they ran all the way into the village. She began to laugh harder as she saw people looking at the flowers and at her in confusion.

Not caring, she began to run, stopping to scoop up the flowers, following the path that Baird had left for her, down to the harbor, past Flynn's restaurant until she found the last flower. Panting, she looked around for the next flower, for a clue, for something.

Aislinn turned in a circle, her arms full of flowers, and then she saw it.

Like a punch to the gut, love overwhelmed her. She sobbed into the flowers, so happy, wanting desperately to see Baird.

Above her, in the second-floor windows that ran the length of Baird's apartment, were her paintings, facing out and lit from below.

The Revelation.

They looked glorious in the windows, with the lighting playing off the waves that both ravaged and loved the painting. He'd bought it. Baird had been the buyer. Aislinn's breath shuddered out of her and she tried to wipe the tears from her face with her arms full of flowers.

"I get it now," Baird's voice said from behind her and Aislinn's entire body stiffened. She turned, her heart full of hope.

"The glow?" Baird gestured to the painting. He looked

tired, just as weary and mussed as she probably looked, Aislinn thought. She wanted to run to him, to hug him, but she sensed he needed to have his say.

"Yes?"

"It's true love, isn't it? The cove glows for true love."

Aislinn's eyes filled with tears again and she blinked against them, Baird turning into a blurry image of color and shape.

"I believe in you, Aislinn. I believe in us. But, I have to ask you, do you?"

Aislinn choked out a sob, and nodded. "I do. I don't think that I fully realized it until I painted this painting. And even then, it wasn't until it was gone that I did. I painted my emotions without being able to see them."

"But you knew…didn't you? What the cove glowing meant?"

"I did. I didn't want to believe it. Wasn't ready to," Aislinn whispered, her body trembling, feeling awful for not telling Baird how she felt.

"Are you ready now?"

"I am, oh, Baird, I'm so sorry. I should have known you wouldn't hurt me like that," Aislinn said and rushed to him, wanting to shout in joy when his arms came around her, crushing the flowers between them.

"I should never have emailed Matthew in the first place. It was a lesson in not needing to know all the answers right away. If I had just waited, I would have had all the answers I needed."

Aislinn blinked up at him through tears and warmth spread through her as he brushed the gentlest of kisses across her lips.

"Can you tell how I feel? Can you?" Aislinn asked, pulling his hand to touch her heart beneath the flowers.

Baird laughed at her. "The Revelation told me everything that I need. Aptly named, at that." He winked at her and then his face sobered. "Feel me, Ash. Go ahead."

Aislinn dropped her mental shields and allowed his love to wash over her, a pure, fresh love that would tarnish and grow stronger with age. The type of love you built a foundation on and would hold up over the years.

The perfect kind.

"I love you," Aislinn whispered against his mouth.

"Aye, I know," Baird laughed at her and Aislinn felt her heart grow fuller for it.

"I'm going to have to buy that painting back from you," Aislinn said, putting her business face on.

"We'll talk."

EPILOGUE

*A*ISLINN LAUGHED AS Morgan lectured a client on not touching the paintings. The girl had proved invaluable in business and Aislinn's career as an artist was thriving.

After the show, there had been such a demand for her paintings that she had agreed to license prints of her work to Red on Green Gallery. The prints had taken off and now she was selling around the world. She'd made more money in a month than she had over the past five years. For once, Aislinn was being smart and squirreling her money away. Her dream was to turn her apartment into a studio and to buy a place nearby.

Or even move in with Baird, she contemplated as she pawed through a folder of black-and-white photographs that she needed to frame. The relationship had blossomed into a full-fledge partnership and they spent their days discussing business, making love, and arguing about how much money Baird would sell The Revelation back to her for.

He was still holding out, she thought with a sniff, though it secretly pleased her that he wanted to keep the paintings.

"Ash, come out here," Baird called from the courtyard.

"Be back in a bit," Aislinn called to Morgan.

She stepped into the sunshine, though a chill had taken over the air. Baird looked every inch the Dr. Yum that Cait still called him in a button-down plaid shirt and dark jeans. He still wore the glasses and Aislinn always did her best to rumple his perfect hair at every chance she got.

"Hi," Aislinn said, beaming up at him.

"Hi, yourself," Baird said and tapped her nose with an envelope he held. "Come for a little stroll with me?"

"Sure," Aislinn said, slipping her hand into his. He tugged her out of the courtyard and across the street to the house next door to her shop. Stopping suddenly, he turned to the front door of the house and raised his hand to knock.

"Baird, the Murphys moved out a month ago," Aislinn said, pulling his arm to stop him from knocking.

Baird turned and smiled at her and opened his palm to show a key. Aislinn tilted her head at him in confusion as he slipped the key in the lock and pushed the bright red door open.

"Come on," Baird said.

"Can we be in here?" Aislinn whispered, not wanting to get in trouble.

"Yes," Baird said simply and led her through a small front foyer to where the first floor opened up into one room, including the kitchen. Aislinn's mouth dropped open.

"What's happened in here? This used to be a bunch of smaller rooms."

"Aye, I had it opened up," Baird said simply and Aislinn turned to him in confusion.

Her mouth dropped open as she saw what stood behind him.

"The Revelation," Aislinn breathed.

It was hung on a long cream brick wall, looking as though it was made for the space, it fit so perfectly. Aislinn whipped her head around to Baird.

"I don't understand. Are you renting?"

Baird handed her the envelope. Aislinn opened it and unfolded the paper. It was a copy of a deed with Baird's name on it.

"You bought it?" Aislinn said, her voice rising to a screech.

"For us. If you'll move in with me."

Aislinn's mouth dropped open and her throat went dry, just for a second.

At her silence, Baird began to stammer, "See, I figured you would like the open space like this, and that you could use the apartment in your old place for a studio. There's a few bedrooms up top and a nice little courtyard. Easy commute to work." Baird shrugged his shoulders and then let out an "oof!" as Aislinn launched herself at him, wrapping her legs around his waist.

"You bought me a house?"

"Us, I bought us a house," Baird clarified with a smile.

"It's perfect," Aislinn breathed against his lips and Baird chuckled.

"Thank God, as I don't think that I can return it."

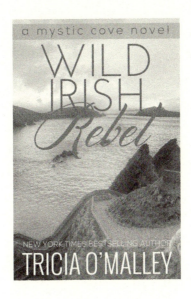

Available now as an e-book, paperback or audiobook!!!

Available from Amazon

The following is an excerpt from Wild Irish Rebel

Book 4 in the Mystic Cove Series

CHAPTER 1

"*S*TOP IT!" Morgan McKenzie awoke on a screech, her throat burning as she clawed at her chest, gasping for air. The beginning of a panic attack burned in her stomach and she struggled to orientate herself.

"Oh no." Morgan jerked her head up and tried to focus her mind away from her panic attack and on the more pressing issue at hand.

That issue being the entire contents of her small studio apartment levitating around her.

Including her bed.

"Okay, just breathe, focus," Morgan ordered herself, desperately trying to lower the objects that hovered around her. She didn't own much in this world and what she did was precious to her. If Morgan shattered her lamp because of a recurring nightmare that she had it would take her at least a week's worth of work to pay for another.

Morgan breathed a small sigh of relief as her bedside table and lamp settled back onto the ground. However, lowering her bed without creating a loud thump for her neighbors below was another thing, and she counted to ten in her head to force herself to concentrate before she timidly lowered the bed gently back onto the ground.

"Oh, this just has to stop," Morgan muttered to herself as she shoved out of bed and walked to the small kitchenette tucked in the corner.

The apartment was tiny and had just barely been within her budget, but Morgan didn't care. It was really nothing more than a large room tucked on the third floor of a small apartment building on the edge of town. But the worn wood floors and curved paned windows had appealed to Morgan and the high ceilings with exposed beams made the space seem larger than it was. With the help of her boss Aislinn, she'd been able to fit a double bed and loveseat, along with a table and two chairs, into the room. Prints of Aislinn's moody seascapes ranged across the brick wall, bringing color and movement to the room. Morgan had secretly delighted in buying a delicate seafoam green comforter for the bed with matching towels for the small bathroom tucked off the kitchen.

It wasn't much, but it was home.

Aside from her van, this was the first space that Morgan could call her own. After years of being unceremoniously moved from foster home to foster home, Morgan had a natural aversion to putting down roots. Until she'd come to Grace's Cove and had found herself able to build friendships for the first time in her life.

And found people who shared similar gifts to hers.

It hadn't been easy for her...growing up without a family, struggling to understand an otherworldly ability that would seemingly act on its own accord. It had gotten so bad that the nuns had periodically tried to exorcize her of demons.

Morgan shuddered as she measured out coffee for her French press.

Talk about instilling deep-rooted insecurities, she thought. Morgan hated the dreams that forced her to relive that time in her life. The nuns had been convinced that they were acting on God's behalf. Only Baird, Aislinn's husband and the resident psychiatrist, had shown her that being tied to a bed and prayed over for hours was really a form of child abuse.

Baird. Morgan breathed out a sigh of relief as she thought of her mild-mannered psychiatrist and friend. He had offered her sessions for free at the request of his wife, and her employer, Aislinn. Her eyes teared up just thinking about how much they had both helped her in such a short time. Morgan was quite certain that she would simply die if she ever disappointed them.

And it wasn't just Baird and Aislinn that had helped her, Morgan thought as she impatiently waited for her coffee to brew. Flynn had taken a chance on her by hiring her to work on his fishing boats with him. His wife Keelin was coming into her own as a healer and she'd been pushing Morgan to spend time with her grandmother, and the greatest healer in all of Ireland, Fiona. Morgan's scalp itched as she thought about meeting with Fiona. She'd spent so long trying to hide her extra abilities that going to Fiona seemed like ripping a bandage off of a wound. She just wasn't ready to tackle that step yet.

Read Wild Irish Rebel today.
Available from Amazon

MS. BITCH

FINDING HAPPINESS IS THE BEST
REVENGE

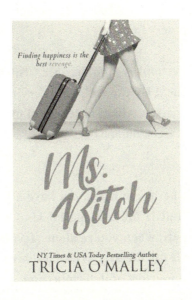

From the outside, it seems thirty-six-year-old Tess Campbell has it all. A happy marriage, a successful career as a novelist, and an exciting cross-country move ahead. Tess has always played by the rules and it seems like life is good.

Except it's not. Life is a bitch. And suddenly so is Tess.

"Ms. Bitch is sunshine in a book! An uplifting story of fighting your way through heartbreak and making your own version of happily-ever-after."
~Ann Charles, USA Today Bestselling Author of the Deadwood Mystery Series

"Authentic and relatable, Ms. Bitch packs an emotional punch. By the end, I was crying happy tears and ready to pack my bags in search of my best life."
-Annabel Chase, author of the Starry Hollow Witches series

"It's easy to be brave when you have a lot of support in your life, but it takes a special kind of courage to forge a new path when you're alone. Tess is the heroine I hope I'll be if my life ever crumbles down around me. Ms. Bitch is a journey of determination, a study in self-love, and a hope for second chances. I could not put it down!"
-Renee George, USA Today Bestselling Author of the Nora Black Midlife Psychic Mysteries

"I don't know where to start listing all the reasons why you should read this book. It's empowering. It's fierce. It's about loving yourself enough to build the life you want. It was honest, and raw, and real and I just...loved it so much!"

— Sara Wylde, author of Fat

AFTERWORD

Ireland holds a special place in my heart – a land of dreamers and for dreamers. There's nothing quite like cozying up next to a fire in a pub and listening to a session or having a cup of tea while the rain mists outside the window. I'll forever be enchanted by her rocky shores and I hope you enjoy this series as much as I enjoyed writing it. Thank you for taking part in my world, I hope that my stories bring you great joy.

Have you read books from my other series? Join our little community by signing up for my newsletter for updates on island-living, fun giveaways, and how to follow me on social media!
http://eepurl.com/1LAiz.

or at my website
www.triciaomalley.com

Please consider leaving a review! Your review helps others to take a chance on my stories. I really appreciate your help!

THE MYSTIC COVE SERIES

ALSO BY TRICIA O'MALLEY

Wild Irish Roots (Novella, Prequel)

Wild Irish Heart

Wild Irish Eyes

Wild Irish Soul

Wild Irish Rebel

Wild Irish Roots: Margaret & Sean

Wild Irish Witch

Wild Irish Grace

Wild Irish Dreamer

Wild Irish Sage

Available in audio, e-book & paperback!

Available from Amazon

"I have read thousands of books and a fair percentage have been romances. Until I read Wild Irish Heart, I never had a book actually make me believe in love."- Amazon Review

THE ISLE OF DESTINY SERIES

ALSO BY TRICIA O'MALLEY

Stone Song

Sword Song

Spear Song

Sphere Song

Available in audio, e-book & paperback!

Available from Amazon

"Love this series. I will read this multiple times. Keeps you on the edge of your seat. It has action, excitement and romance all in one series."- Amazon Review

AUTHOR'S NOTE

Thank you for taking a chance on my books; it means the world to me. Writing novels came by way of a tragedy that turned into something beautiful and larger than itself (see: *The Stolen Dog*). Since that time, I've changed my career, put it all on the line, and followed my heart.

Thank you for taking part in the worlds I have created; I hope you enjoy it.

I would be honored if you left a review online. It helps other readers to take a chance on my work.

As always, you can reach me at
info@triciaomalley.com
or feel free to visit my website at
www.triciaomalley.com.

AUTHOR'S ACKNOWLEDGEMENT

First, and foremost, I'd like to thank my family and friends for their constant support, advice, and ideas. You've all proven to make a difference on my path. And, to my beta readers, I love you for all of your support and fascinating feedback!

And last, but never least, my two constant companions as I struggle through words on my computer each day - Briggs and Blue.

Made in the USA
Monee, IL
24 March 2021

63685055R00166